LAWTON COOP WAS CORNERED

There was a man on each side of him and the tough called Heavy in front.

"This here's Baylor Coop's brother," Heavy said to the crowd in the El Raton. "We can't let 'im walk out of here."

"You'll be the first to die," Lawton said, looking straight at Heavy. His guts were knotted with fear and his knees wanted to tremble, but he couldn't let it show. "Draw or git!"

Heavy's hand hovered over his sixgun, but he didn't draw. This was Lawton Coop, brother of Baylor Coop, the cowboy who'd outdrawn and outshot two men right here on the same spot. Finally his hand dropped to his side. "You Coops are gunfighters. Just goddamn gunfighters."

Lawton said, "Damn right."

GUNSMOKE JUSTICE

Doyle Trent

ZEBRA BOOKS
KENSINGTON PUBLISHING CORP.

ZEBRA BOOKS

are published by

Kensington Publishing Corp.
475 Park Avenue South
New York, NY 10016

First printing: February, 1989

Printed in the United States of America

Chapter One

Baylor Coop was missing. He was either dead or badly hurt.

"Somethin's happened," his old ma said. "I can feel it. Go find him, Lawton. Go up to Colorado and find your brother."

So Lawton Coop was heading due north, following the mountain branch of the Santa Fe Trail where the traveling was easy. Along the way he passed half a dozen ox wagons going south with heavy loads of trade goods, and nine or ten wagons carrying families north to Colorado Territory.

Colorado, where rich farming and grazing land was free.

Baylor had been gone over a year now, and the last letter his mother got from him was posted nine months ago in Pueblo, Territory of Colorado. Baylor was wild, full of adventure, afraid of nothing or nobody. But even when he was in the war, he wrote home to his mother once a week.

Lawton had tried to ease her worries. "If there ever was a man who could take care of himself, Mom, it's Baylor. He got through the war, didn't he? And with Mary about to calve and everything . . ."

His mother's body was thin and worn from the task of raising two ornery teenage boys after their dad was killed by the Apaches. She had raised them and hung on to the

5

100,000 acres of arid salt grass and mesquite in Southern New Mexico Territory. Sometimes she could afford to hire help, sometimes she couldn't. Finally the boys were grown, and the ranch was making a decent living. She no longer had to work so hard. But now, sitting at the kitchen table, her face in her hands, she was fighting back tears.

"Find him, Lawton. Or find out what happened to him."

And when the spring calf roundup was over he'd saddled up and kissed Mary goodbye, promising to be back before their first child was born.

Riding a good stout dun horse and leading a bay pack horse, two of the best horses on the Coop family's Circle C Ranch, he averaged a good forty miles a day. He had been riding four days when he came within sight of the Raton Mountains.

The country here was mostly gentle hills with purple mountains to the west and flat-topped, steep-sided mesas to the east. Yucca was everywhere, its long, jagged green leaves and columns of bell-shaped pods pointing skyward. Soap-weeds, most folks called them. Good grass was plentiful. Good cattle country. In the summer, anyway.

The trail was easy to follow. Thousands of wagon wheels and hooves had beaten down the grass, leaving ruts among the yucca. Rain and snowmelt had eroded the ruts so deep in places that the wagons had stayed out of them, making new ruts, running parallel.

Lawton wore the wide-brim hat and high-heeled boots of a cattleman. A pair of leather chaps hung across the saddle in front of him, stirring in the breeze. He didn't need chaps in the kind of country he was riding through, and the damned things were too warm anyway.

He camped out that night at the foot of the mountains, next to a creek that poured out of a canyon. Raton Creek, he believed. His horses were used to being hobbled and sidelined and he didn't have to worry about them running off or hurting themselves trying to run off. Grass was stirrup high. They could eat and rest.

The gurgling of the creek was pleasant to his ears as he lay in his bed on a thin mattress with a long tarp under it and folded back over him. Two blankets and a pillow. He kept the Spencer carbine beside his bed and the Army Colt six-shooter under the tarp with him.

Baylor had picked up the Spencer, a Yankee gun, on a battlefield somewhere in Georgia and brought it home. At first they couldn't buy the .52-caliber cartridges it fired. Then on a trip up to Santa Fe, Lawton had found some in a gun shop and bought two hundred rounds to take back to his brother.

Baylor had appreciated that, and he and Lawton fired about a hundred rounds with the gun just for the fun of it. But—and now Lawton's mood turned dark and heavy when he remembered—Baylor had given the gun up, just as he'd promised.

It was over a horse race. Baylor believed his four-year-old sorrel gelding could outrun any horse in the territory for half a mile. Lawton believed his long-backed gray could cover a half-mile faster. They made a bet. For the first five hundred yards the sorrel was in the lead, but just before they got to the half-mile mark the gray nosed ahead.

Lawton could remember the hurt in Baylor's eyes when he'd handed the gun over. It was one of his proudest possessions. Now Lawton squinched his eyes shut and tried to blot out the memory.

He wished he hadn't won that race.

Would he find Baylor sick somewhere, too sick to write? Or would he find a grave? Men died or were killed and were buried wherever the grave digging was easy. Sometimes their kin never knew what happened to them.

The road over the Raton Mountains was a rough one, rocky, steep, and so narrow most of the way that one wagon couldn't pass another. Lawton could see where men had used blasting powder, picks, shovels and fresnos to build the road. It took cross-cut saws, axes and draw knives to cut down the big timbers, skin the bark off and build the bridges. A hell of a lot of work and money. His horses, coming from the sandy country in the Pecos Valley, were not shod, and he worried that they would get sorefooted in the rocky mountains. He let them take their time and pick their way over the rocks.

It would have been cheaper to take the Trinchera Pass to the east. He'd been told about the toll gate at the top of the Raton Mountains. But the Trinchera was out of his way, and he wanted to finish his mission and get back home. Back to Mary, his wife of fourteen months, at least eight months pregnant.

Halfway up he came to a wide spot near the creek where travelers had camped many times, a place where wagons could pass. He let his horses drink and was moving on when he met a man on horseback coming down. The man wore dirty, wrinkled wool clothes. His bush beard under a floppy black hat was tobacco-stained. He rode a long-legged breed of a horse that had come from the east. Both men reined up.

"Morning," Lawton said.

"Mornin'." The man sat his saddle on one hind cheek. "Seen anything on wheels back thar?"

"Not today. Passed a couple of wagons yesterday, about the middle of the morning. You looking for somebody?"

"Naw." He spat a stream of tobacco juice on the opposite side of his horse. "I'm leadin' the way for a dozen mule wagons comin' from Denver, and thar's only a couple of turnouts up thar whar wagons can pass one another."

"I see," Lawton said. "You have to stop any wagons coming up or go back and stop your wagons."

"Yup. But if you ain't seen any today, I reckon we're safe."

"How far to the top of these hills?"

"Not far. 'Bout five mile, I'd cal'clate. Be ready to pay. Old

8

Wootton's got a gate up thar and he ain't lettin' nobody through without payin'."

"I heard about that." Lawton glanced around him. "From the looks of this road, I'd say he's earned anything he can collect."

"That's what he says, and he don't take no shit from nobody. You either pay 'im or you turn around."

Lawton grinned a slow grin. "I'm not planning to argue with him."

"There's talk up in Denver that somebody's gonna build a railroad down here in a few years. That'll put us mule skinners out of business."

"Yep," Lawton allowed, picking up his reins, "it's bound to happen. Some day the railroads will be here."

A half-hour later he met a string of twelve heavy freight wagons, drawn by six mules to the wagon. They passed him in a place where one side of the road went straight up and the other side dropped straight down into the creek. He had to stop his horses and crowd them up against the rock wall to let the wagons pass. The teamsters kept one foot on the brake handles, ready to kick on the brakes where the road was steep.

In another half-hour he topped a long hill and stopped to let his horses blow. Huge boulders lined the road on each side. Beyond the boulders pine and spruce trees towered above the short cedars. A quarter mile ahead he saw three buildings, all made of timbers and rocks. There were a two-story building, a small shack and a barn. And there was a pole gate across the road.

"WOOO" said a hand-painted sign hanging from the gate. Lawton would have bet, when he got close enough to read it, that it was misspelled. He whoaed at the gate. Another sign, this one over the door to the shack, read: GROSERIES.

The man who came out of the shack was big. The biggest man Lawton had ever seen. He stood six feet four, at least, and he must have weighed 240 or maybe even 250 pounds.

He wasn't fat, either, and he looked like he could wrestle a bear and win.

"Light and rest your saddle," the man said pleasantly. "Coffee's on."

Dismounting, Lawton said, "I could use some coffee. Can't stay, however. How much are you gonna charge me to go through that gate?"

"Two bits." The man wore baggy wool pants held up with red suspenders. His gray beard looked as if it had been trimmed with sheep shears, and his shaggy eyebrows had obviously never been trimmed.

"Are you Mr. Wootton?"

"Riches Lacy Wootton is the name. Some folks call me Uncle Dick."

Digging into his pants pocket, Lawton pulled out a silver coin. "Well, Mr. Wootton, I'll bet those mule skinners are more than happy to pay for the use of your road. A man on a horse doesn't really need it though."

"You're usin' it."

Lawton had already decided he was going to pay. The last thing he wanted was an argument. He paid.

"Where you headed? Not that it's any of my business."

"Pueblo first, and then I don't know. I'm looking for a man. Name of Coop. Baylor Coop. I don't suppose you ever heard of him."

The bushy eyebrows came together and the eyes squinted at Lawton. "You a kin?"

"I am."

"Well, I'd keep it to myself, if I was you."

"Why would I do that?"

"I never met the man, but I heered of 'im. A deputy shurff from Las Animas County came through here last fall or early winter, I disremember which, lookin' for a man of that name."

A sudden chill ran up Lawton's back, and he stared hard

at the bearded one. A lawman looking for Baylor? This wasn't right. Something was terribly wrong.

He said, "A deputy sheriff? Why?"

"Said a gent name of Baylor Coop was wanted over to Trinidad for murder, robbery, jailbreak and just about ever' crime there is."

Chapter Two

It ate on him. As he rode down the pass, down the narrow road, between the boulders and the cedar and piñon trees, it gnawed at his guts. Murder? If Baylor had killed anyone it was in self-defense. Robbery? No sir. Not Baylor. Jail break? Well, if he was locked up for a crime he didn't commit, he might bust out.

Baylor was the younger brother, and the good-looking one, with his dad's thick curly hair and bright blue eyes, the one who'd volunteered to fight for the Confederacy. Tough as a boot, he could handle a gun with the best of them, and would rather be hurt bad, even shot, than to run from a fight. But he was as honest as they made them. His mother had seen to that.

"Ain't nothin' worse than a thief," she had said, often. "And a man that cain't keep his word ain't no man a-tall."

But where was Baylor? If a deputy sheriff was looking for him, he must have got away. Or did they catch him? Was he dead? Or was he in prison somewhere?

He was either dead or in prison. Otherwise he would have written to his mother. If he was in prison, he maybe wouldn't want anyone to know, and he wouldn't write. But no, they didn't put men in prison for murder. Not robbery murder. Baylor had to be dead. Buried somewhere near Trinidad.

12

just over the New Mexico border. Lawton would have to find the grave and find out what had happened.

And—his guts twisted when he thought about it—go back home and tell his mother.

The town of Trinidad looked as if it belonged farther south. Way south. It had the appearance of a Mexican village, with its adobe huts, and ragged brown-faced children playing in the streets. And dogs. Always dogs. The Mexicans were the first to settle in New Mexico and Texas, but he didn't realize they'd come this far north. But then Lawton had never before been this far north. He could speak a little Spanish, but he'd rather speak English. The town sat at the end of a long flat-topped hill coming from the west. Another hill on the south rose almost straight up.

He rode across a wide bridge, and he guessed that the river under it was the Picketwire. The adobe huts were scattered with dusty streets, yucca and wild grasses between them. One street, wider than the others, had a hand-painted sign on a pole, and it was lined on one side with a board sidewalk. "Commerce Street." It was well named. The buildings on the north side were commercial buildings, built of rough lumber with false fronts. A hotel, two saloons, a mercantile. There were more. And a bank. A bank? Yeah, that's what the sign said. Merchants Bank of Las Animas County.

Commerce Street was quiet. Siesta time. Lawton's stomach reminded him he hadn't stopped for dinner. He'd take care of that if he could find a café. That is, after he'd cared for his horses. Riding down the street, he read the signs in the windows and saw a café. The Trinchera Eatery. Fine Foods. That was on a corner. Across the street was a laundry, a vacant weed-grown lot, and a long, narrow brick building with a flat roof and high windows. A sign on its plank door said: THE LAS ANIMAS GAZETTE. A newspaper? Yep. The message on one of the windows was in gold script, and it said James C. Gordon was the publisher and editor.

13

A light spring wagon went by in the opposite direction, and the man, in rancher's clothes, merely nodded at Lawton. Smoke rose from a steam plant of some kind on the west side of town. Probably a sawmill with a steam-powered saw. On the east, ahead of him, was a new building that looked to be the biggest building in town. Covered at least a thousand square feet and made of brick and rock. Before he got to it, he saw the sheriff's office.

Sheriff. That's all the sign painted on the small window said. A hitchrack made of skinned pine poles was planted in front of it.

Lawton swung down and wrapped the reins around the horizontal pole. The door was locked. He knocked. No answer. Knocked again, louder.

"He ain't there."

Lawton turned to see a man in denim overalls held up by suspenders. A pillbox cap sat crookedly on his head. The man stood on the sidewalk scratching a week's growth of beard.

"He's to home. Gen'ly comes back about two o'clock."

"Oh," said Lawton. "What's his name?"

"Willard. Horace Willard. Just got elected last winter."

"Well, thanks. Is the café open?"

"Gen'ly is. They'll gen'ly feed a feller if he's got money."

"Is there a livery barn or someplace I can put up my horses?"

"There's a wagon camp east a ways and two streets north. Walkin' distance. They'll put you up."

"Well, thanks."

"Come far?"

"From the Pecos Valley in New Mexico. Five days."

"Your horses look like they've come a ways."

"Yeah, they're a little sorefooted. We don't shoe horses where I come from. I'm gonna have to let them rest a few days."

Another pedestrian, a small thin man in a Prince Albert

coat with a cravat at the throat, went into the newspaper office. Two women in long dresses and poke bonnets went by. The men stepped aside politely to give them room on the sidewalk.

"They'll put you up at the wagon camp. Straight north and then east. Can't miss 'er."

The wagon camp was like others he'd seen. It covered two acres of bare ground. One side was lined with stalls built of logs, with poles between each stall. Horses munched hay in four of the stalls. The flies, big black horse flies, were bad in the afternoon heat, and the horses were constantly switching their tails, stamping their feet, kicking at flies on their bellies and shivering their hides, trying to fight them off. Two covered wagons were parked next to the stalls. The other side of the lot was lined with a half-dozen small one-room log shacks. A pimply-faced kid in overalls was raking manure out of a stall. Lawton reined over.

"Where can I find the proprietor?" he asked.

The boy, tall, thin, leaned against his manure rake and looked past him. "Yonder." He nodded in the direction of the cabins. "He's in Number One."

"Obliged." At the cabin with a number one painted on the plank door, he dismounted, dropped the reins and knocked on the door. Knocked again, and waited.

Must be a Mexican taking his siesta, Lawton thought. He knocked again. Finally the door opened and a short man wearing baggy pants and a dirty undershirt stood there. "Yeah?" He was neither friendly nor unfriendly.

"I'm looking for a place to put up for the night. Me and two horses."

"Two bits for you and two bits for the horses. All the hay you want. Good mountain meadow hay."

Lawton paid for a day and night and said he might have to stay longer. He unsaddled his horses, watered them at a steel tank, put them in stalls and fed them hay, good green hay, a kind of grass he'd never seen before. He carried his bedroll and pack panniers into cabin number four, then walked back down the street to the café.

He was the only customer, and the man behind the long wooden counter looked as if he'd just awakened from a nap. Bleary-eyed, he said Lawton would have to settle for a cold beef sandwich. Hadn't started cooking supper yet. A sandwich would be fine, Lawton said. As he ate it, he recalled the advice of Mr. Wootton. Uncle Dick Wootton. Baylor Coop wasn't popular in Trinidad, and his brother wouldn't be welcomed with open arms. Should he keep his identity to himself?

By the time he finished his sandwich, he'd made up his mind. Baylor might have done something illegal, but he, by God, hadn't done anything disgraceful. There was some-times a hell of a difference. No, he'd tell the popeyed world who he was and what he'd come for. And if anybody didn't like it, well, they'd just have to fight about it. Baylor was the faster of the two brothers with a gun, but Lawton had practiced with him, and if he had to, he could fight.

Only when he thought of Mary, a couple of weeks from calving, he hoped to hell he wouldn't have to.

The sheriff's office was unlocked so Lawton walked in. It was a two-room building with thick adobe walls, and one of the rooms was a jail. A door with steel bars separated it from the front room. The jail's one occupant lay on a dirty mattress on a wooden bunk and snored like a groaning bull. The place stank of bad whiskey, vomit and human feces.

"Hello," Lawton said.

The snoring continued. No one else was around. "Hello." The door opened and a man walked in behind Lawton, carrying a bucket. He was gray-haired with a gray moustache, about six feet even, an inch taller than Lawton, and he was heavier. He wore new denim pants and a six-gun low on his right hip. His hat was wide in the brim, flat on top and looked to be nearly new. A big silver star was pinned to his shirt pocket.

"Are you the sheriff?"

"I am. Horace Willard, sheriff of Las Animas County." He set the bucket on the floor. "Goddamn swamper. Can't depend on him. I didn't get elected to this job so I could carry out the shit. Who are you and what do you want?"

"My name is Lawton Coop."

Horace Willard's eyes narrowed and his mouth tightened under the gray moustache. "The hell you beller. You're not . . . ?"

Lawton didn't let him finish. "That's right. I'm the brother of Baylor Coop."

The two men stared at each other for a long moment, then, "I don't suppose you happen to know where Baylor Coop is?"

The question eased Lawton's worries a little. If the sheriff didn't know where Baylor was, then Baylor must be alive. A fugitive from justice, but alive.

"No sir, I don't. I came here to try to find him."

The sheriff sat in a wooden chair at a scarred wooden desk and let his eyes rove over Lawton from top to bottom and back up. Lawton was average-looking, maybe an inch above average in height, slender, but strong, clean-shaven, sandy hair, blue eyes with squint wrinkles and a jaw that was strong but not pugnacious. The sheriff's eyes stopped for two seconds on the Colt six-gun. The gun rode high on Lawton's hip. High for comfort, not for a fast draw.

"I don't know whether to believe you or not, but I'm inclined to believe you. If you knew where Baylor Coop is and was sharing in the loot, you sure as hell wouldn't be here."

"Loot? What loot?"

The pale blue eyes studied Lawton's face. Finally, he drawled, "What loot? Well, sir, I'll tell you what loot. Bank loot. Your brother robbed the bank and took every dollar in it. He left a lot of folks around here flat busted, and they ain't too happy about it."

17

"Huh-uh." Lawton was shaking his head. "I don't believe it. Not Baylor."

"It was him, all right. And that ain't all. He killed Sheriff Bill Spates. Shot him right through the heart."

Lawton looked into the sheriff's eyes, hoping to see some sign of uncertainty, some sign of weakness. There was none. The sheriff was sure of what he was saying. All Lawton could do was sputter, "Huh-uh. Not Baylor. There's a mistake here somewhere. Baylor wouldn't do anything like that. Huh-uh."

"You think I'm joking? Look here." Willard yanked open a desk drawer and took out a sheet of paper. He handed it to Lawton.

"Wanted," it read. "Baylor Coop. Tinhorn gambler, aquaphobiac, thief, murderer, jail breaker, macquereau, bank robber, land grabber, misotonsorist, satyriasist, and liar." It gave Baylor's description: "Middle twenties, six feet one inch, 185 pounds, dark hair and blue eyes."

Near the bottom, in big black letters, it said, "Reward. Five Hundred Dollars." And below that:

"Dead or Alive."

Chapter Three

The bed had been slept in since the sheets had been washed. No telling how many or what kind of people had slept in it. Lawton knew that some of the public beds were lousy with livestock—the kind with legs on both sides. Little, crawly, biting livestock. He unrolled his own bed on the floor and slept in it. The cabin in the wagon camp contained an iron bedstead with a mattress, two blankets and two muslin sheets, nails in the walls to hang clothes on, and a washstand with a tin basin on it and a small mirror over that. There was also a small wood-burning stove with long-dead ashes in it.

Should have checked into the hotel. He decided he'd leave his horses here next day and sleep in the hotel. Had to be a better room than this.

Baylor, where was Baylor sleeping? Baylor was hiding from the law. Robbed a bank and killed a lawman. Accused of everything imaginable. What the hell is a misotonsorist? And a satyriasist? Hell, there probably are no such things. Those are just words somebody read somewhere and put on the wanted poster to make Baylor look worse than he was.

Whoever wrote the message on that poster wasn't trying to be fair and honest.

In fact, nothing about this whole sorry mess was fair and honest. It stunk. It stunk worse than that town jail.

19

Sure, Baylor was a scrapper. Liked a good fight. As kids Baylor and Lawton had fought all the time. They fought like cats and dogs over everything that came up. Mrs. Coop had scolded them, whipped them with their dead father's razor strop, pleaded with them, but still they fought. Best of friends one minute and fighting the next. Hell, Lawton had to grin to himself as he lay in his bed with his hands under his head and recalled it all, they liked to fight.

Then—Lawton's grin vanished and an unpleasant memory came to his mind—there was the last fight. It was Lawton's fault. He was nineteen and Baylor was seventeen. Until then, Lawton was the older and the bigger, and Baylor was always accusing him of taking an unfair advantage of his size. But that fight ended it.

They had been prowling pastures, looking for cattle that needed doctoring. It was a dry year and the screw worms were bad. Baylor carried a long-bladed knife in a small boot fastened to the back rigging rings on his saddle, and a pint whiskey bottle of pine tar. The bottle was wrapped with black tape to keep it from breaking, and it was carried in a pouch made from the top of a worn-out boot. All day, Baylor had been kidding Lawton about something. He couldn't remember what. But by the time they found the wormy cow, he had had enough of it. The cow carried a wound in her left side, and the wound was full of screw worms—the little larva that got into a wound and ate away like maggots. Only they ate on live animals. Ate them alive.

Baylor took his rope down, tied the end hard and fast to his saddle horn and shook out a loop. Lawton got his rope ready. The cow ran like a deer and gave their horses a good race before Baylor's loop shot out and snagged both horns. His horse sat back on the rope and the cow was jerked around hard. She didn't like that and took after Baylor's horse, trying to hook him with her long horns. But Lawton had his loop whirling over his head and was right behind and to the left of her. He swung his loop over the cow's right hip,

20

setting a trap for the hind feet.

And then the cow was stretched out between two horses, completely helpless.

While Lawton stayed on his horse, backing him to keep the heel rope tight, Baylor got down and went to work. Using the long-bladed knife, he scraped the worms out of the wound, then smeared the wound with pine tar. While he worked, he spoke to the cow. "There, old lady. You don't know it, but we saved you from a hell of a lot of misery. I'm gonna take this rope off your horns and we're gonna turn you loose, so don't get any ideas like maybe showing your gratitude by punching holes in me."

He took his rope off the cow's horns, depending on his older brother to keep the heel loop tight so the cow couldn't get up until he was safely on his horse.

But Lawton, feeling the sting of the rawhiding he'd taken all day, saw a chance to get even. He rode forward, slacking up on the rope. The cow jumped up, kicked off the heel loop and went after Baylor.

"Oh, my God," Lawton said to himself when he realized what he'd done. He yelled a warning. Baylor looked back, saw the cow bearing down on him, saw he couldn't get on his horse, and hit the ground. Flat. The cow was on him, trying to prod a horn into him. Baylor hugged the ground, cursing.

"Oh, Lord," Lawton muttered. He slapped spurs to his mount and charged the cow. His horse rammed the cow broadside, knocking her down. The horse stumbled over her, but kept its balance and stayed right-side-up. Next the cow took after Lawton's horse, giving Baylor a chance to get mounted. Then the horses outran the cow and left her behind, with her head up, a kink in her tail, shaking her horns, ready to fight anything she could catch.

The two brothers rode silently over a rise and down into a sandy draw. There Baylor stopped. He spoke two words:

"Git down."

How they fought. Fists, feet, teeth, knees. They fought

until they both were so winded and wounded they couldn't get to their feet. Gasping for breath, they lay on the sand, bleeding. Baylor's left eye was closed, and blood poured from his nose. Lawton's right eye was swelling fast, and a cut lip dripped blood onto his shirt. His fists were skinned and bleeding. Baylor's too.

They gasped and heaved, and finally Baylor got to his knees. By sheer willpower, Lawton got to his knees too. Neither had the strength to stand, but they swung punches, hitting each other. Hurting.

Both fell back at the same time, unable to move. They lay on their backs with their lungs pounding and their faces and hands numb. For a long time they lay there. The sky swirled overhead and the ground trembled. Lawton thought his heart was going to jump out of his chest where it would have more room. He thought he was going to die.

Gasping, coughing, heaving.

Gradually, the sky stopped moving. Breathing was coming easier. Eventually, Lawton was able to turn his head and look at his brother. He tried to speak, but only mumbled through split lips. He gasped, and tried again.

"It . . . was estupido . . . what I did, Bay. It's . . . my . . . fault."

Flat on his back, Baylor turned his head too, and spoke in the same halting fashion. "Tell me . . . something . . . Law. Can you still whup . . . me?"

"No. I can't, Bay. You're . . . outgrowing . . . me. I can't whup you . . . no more."

It was their last fight. Which was lucky for Lawton, because Baylor kept on growing until he was two inches taller and about twenty pounds heavier. Oh, they kidded each other about everything that came up, especially girls, and they bet against each other on horse races. But there was nothing they wouldn't do for each other.

And they worshipped their poor, tired old mother.

*   *   *

22

Breakfast at the café was hotcakes with thick molasses, bacon and coffee. Condensed milk for the coffee was offered, but Lawton drank his black. Four other men sat at the plank counter, two of them cowboys. Their hats were a little broader in the brim than Lawton's and their boots had higher heels, but otherwise they dressed pretty much the same. Except that they wore no guns. He'd noticed, before he went into the café, that the two horses tied to a hitchrail in front carried saddles with three-quarter riggings. In the South, where he was from, cowboys all rode saddles with rim-fire double riggings.

They were stealing glances his way, wondering what outfit he rode for or where he was from, and finally, one of them, a short man with a square jaw, just had to find out.

"Purty day, ain't it? Shore could use some rain though."

"Yep, nice day. Didn't see a cloud in the sky this morning."

"Bet you're from Texas."

Lawton grinned. "You'd miss your bet, but you're close. New Mexico Territory. The Pecos Valley."

"I've heard of the Pecos River. Quicksandy as hell, ain't she?"

"In some places sometimes."

"You working around here?"

"Naw. Just passing through. Looks like good grass country."

"Over to the west is some of the best grass in the world in the summer, but the snow gets purty deep sometimes in the winter."

"I hear land is free for the taking? Is that right?"

"Naw. The best of it belongs to the Maxwell."

"The Maxwell? I've heard of the Maxwell Land Grant. Is that it?"

"Yeah, it belonged to a Mexican named Maxwell, but he sold it."

"I read somewhere that the United States Congress said he could do that."

"That it did, and the squatters are havin' to get off, and

23

they don't like it one damned bit."

The other cowboy, a thin man with a smooth-shaven face and high cheekbones, got into the conversation. "Been some folks killed over that land. The Maxwells claimed all along it belonged to them, but the squatters didn't believe it and put up their shacks and plowed up the land wherever they felt like it."

Lawton cleaned his plate and took a sip of coffee. "I've seen that happen in the Pecos Valley. They thought it was there for anybody that wanted to plant a crop. But there wasn't much trouble. Can't grow anything there anyway. It takes sixty acres to graze a cow and calf."

The thin one chuckled. "They was growin' some spuds and carrots and turnips and stuff like that over there, but the Maxwell wanted 'em off and hired some gun toughs to run 'em off."

"There were people killed, you say?"

"Yep. Some of the nesters ain't givin' up. The Maxwell runs cattle over there and the sodbusters think ever' cowboy is their mortal enemy."

"Yeah," the short one said, "I rode for the Maxwell for a couple months last summer, but I didn't like makin' war on hard-workin' folks so I rolled up my bed and hauled my freight out of there."

Lawton shook his head sadly. "Too bad. Who're you working for now?"

"The O.T. Slim and me took a couple days off to see the city lights."

Draining his coffee cup, Lawton stood, unbuttoned his shirt pocket and reached for his money roll. "Well, you boys have fun and stay out of jail. That sheriff looks like he could eat cowboys for breakfast."

"Old Willard? He's all right. But we're not packin' iron. It's easier to stay out of trouble that way."

Maybe, Lawton thought as he stood on the sidewalk, they had the right idea. Leave your guns at home and stay out of trouble. If he left his Colt in the cabin at the wagon camp, maybe folks would realize his intentions were peaceful. Even though he was Baylor Coop's brother. Yeah, that's what he'd do.

Before he left the cabin, he made certain the padlock was clamped shut, and he had the key in his pocket. He also made certain his two horses were fed and watered. He felt strange without a gun on his hip, kind of lopsided. He felt strange walking so much, too. He had seldom walked farther than from the house to the corrals. Aw well, do him good to stretch his legs now and then. So walk. Walk where?

Back to the sheriff's office. Find out what the present sheriff knew about the old one and the bank robbery. Pedestrian traffic was picking up. Mostly Mexicans. Wagon traffic was still light. Trinidad seemed to be a trade town more than anything else. A place to buy supplies. A stopping place on the Santa Fe Trail. He walked past the newspaper building, paused, thought it over, turned and went in.

She was one of the prettiest girls he had ever seen. Except for Mary she was the prettiest. She was standing by the high window, standing on her toes to look out when he came through the door. About five-four, slender, dark brown hair, wide brown eyes. Nice face. A small dimple on her chin. Behind her was a flatbed press with a big roller on the end. Two wooden cases of lead type stood on wooden legs. A man was setting type by hand.

"Yes sir," she said pleasantly. "How are you this fine morning?"

Damn, she was pretty.

"Uh, I was wondering," Lawton began, not knowing what to say. "I was wondering if, uh . . . Let me introduce myself. My name is Lawton Coop." He paused to see if the name got a reaction. It did.

"Coop?" She was suddenly flustered. "Lawton Coop?"

"Yes, ma'am, I . . ."

"You're Baylor Coop's brother?" Her brown eyes were wide, and her left hand went to her throat.

"Yes, ma'am. Do you know my brother?"

"Why, I, uh . . ." She was trying to decide how to answer. He could see that. "Why, uh, yes, I, uh was slightly acquainted with him."

He had to grin. Wouldn't you know it. She was one of the prettiest girls in the West, and you could bet old Bay would make himself known to her. Bay liked the girls and the girls liked Bay. "Miss, I'm trying to find my brother. I'd sure like to know what happened to him. I was wondering if maybe the newspaper printed the news about the robbery he was supposed to have done. And the murder."

"Why yes." She glanced at the man in the back. He looked up, curious. Lawton had seen him before. He was the man in the Prince Albert coat who had entered the newspaper office the day before. Now he had his coat off and was wearing an ink-smudged apron and some half-lens glasses low on his nose. "Of course," the girl went on, her voice picking up strength, "we print the news. We sent the story by telegraph to Denver and it was printed in the Denver newspapers." She seemed to be proud of that.

"Would you happen to have the back, uh, issues or whatever you call them?"

"Yes, we do. We have copies of every newspaper we've printed."

"Can I, uh, I'd sure like to read about what happened."

"Well, I . . ." She turned her head and spoke in a loud voice to the man in back, "Daddy, this gentleman says he is Baylor Coop's brother."

The man wiped his hands on the apron and came forward. "Yes sir? You're a relative of Mr. Coop?" He looked over his glasses at Lawton, and he didn't seem unfriendly.

Lawton didn't know whether to offer his hand to the man or not. He decided to try it. "My name is Lawton Coop, sir.

ame up here from the Pecos Valley to find my brother or ind out what happened to him."

His hand was taken, given two shakes and dropped. "I am James C. Gordon, editor and publisher. This is my daughter, Annie."

"I'm pleased to meet you." He repeated his request.

"Yes, you may," Mr. Gordon said. "But I must insist that ou read the paper here. We have no copies to spare."

"That will be fine, Mr. Gordon, and I sure do appreciate it."

The girl was studying his face, trying to find a similarity etween him and Baylor Coop. Mr. Gordon went to a huge olltop desk and began searching through the drawers. The girl continued studying Lawton's face. He met her gaze.

"Did you know my brother well, Miss Gordon?"

"Not very well."

"Would you mind telling me what you did know about im?"

"I met him once or twice, and the last time he told me he'd ought some land. Six hundred acres, he said."

"He did?" This was news, something he hadn't expected. Where?"

"Over on the Maxwell."

Uh-oh. A bell went off in Lawton's mind. Not a bell, a oud clank. On the Maxwell. According to what he'd heard t breakfast, this was trouble. This was the kind of trouble hat led to shooting and killing.

Baylor was mixed up in it.

Chapter Four

The story was all there, all anyone could expect. It was Special Edition, which no doubt carried the biggest news story in the town that year. The editor and his daughter had obviously worked all night to get the newspaper printed by early morning. Dated October 4, 1869, it read:

The Merchants Bank of Las Animas County was robbed early last night and Sheriff William S. Spates was murdered. Bank President Benjamin Mock identified the robber and killer as one Baylor Coop, who was already wanted in Trinidad for jailbreak. Mr. Mock said every dollar in the bank's safe was taken.

In an interview by the Las Animas Gazette, Mr. Mock related that he was preparing to retire for the night at his home on the west side when he heard a loud knocking on the door. Mr. Mock's housekeeper, Mrs. Alfred Willis, was preparing to leave for the night, and it was she who opened the door. Mrs. Willis related she recognized Baylor Coop, and when Mr. Mock came to the door Mr. Coop threatened him with a large revolver. The perpetrator ordered Mr. Mock to accompany him to the bank and there ordered him

28

to open the safe.

Mr. Mock stated that he had to comply with the robber's orders or be shot to death. The perpetrator then took all the money from the safe except for some silver change, and was preparing to leave when Sheriff Spates entered through the bank's door, which Mr. Mock and the robber had inadvertently left open. Sheriff Spates ordered the robber to throw up his hands, but the robber whirled around and fired, the bullet striking Sheriff Spates directly in the heart.

Mr. Mock said the robber ran out of the bank, going south, carrying the stolen bank money in a flour sack. He has not been seen since.

Mr. Mock related he is convinced that the robber and killer was Baylor Coop, one of the homesteaders who was arrested last month for refusing to obey the sheriff's orders and abandon land that belongs to the Maxwell Land Company. Mr. Mock is in charge of sales for the land company, and is familiar with the trouble the sheriff is having persuading the illegal migrants to abandon the company's land and take up homesteads elsewhere.

After his arrest, Mr. Coop managed to escape from the jail and was not seen in this vicinity again until last night. Mr. Coop, an itinerant, was involved in another homicide in which two men were killed earlier last month, allegedly over a poker game. He was not arrested at the time because witnesses said the two dead men, also itinerants, instigated the altercation which resulted in the shooting. Nothing is known about Mr. Coop, or where he came from or where he went. Townsmen told Deputy Sheriff William Core that Mr. Coop came to Trinidad from Pueblo, and had been in the goldfields near Pikes Peak.

As of this writing, Deputy Core has organized a large posse and is going south in hopes of locating

Mr. Coop and bringing him to justice. Mr. Mock said the bank has no funds now to reimburse the depositors, and he fears that unless Mr. Coop is located, the funds have been lost forever. Some twenty or thirty townsmen have joined in the manhunt.

Lawton Coop sat in the editor's chair at the rolltop desk and read the story twice. He refolded the paper and frowned at the floor, shaking his head sadly. "I don't believe it," he muttered. "It can't be."

"Pardon me, sir?" It was the girl speaking.

He looked up at her, still shaking his head, pain in his eyes. "It's not true. Baylor is not a thief. If he killed anyone it was self-defense. There's a mistake here."

"Mr. Mock identified him positively. He recognized Baylor Coop after the trouble he had on the Maxwell. Mrs. Willis also identified him."

James C. Gordon came over and stood beside his daughter. "We worked all night and far into the morning, setting type as fast as our fingers could go, getting the story into print. Because of our labors, no one in Las Animas County had to guess what happened."

Lawton stood. "I know you worked hard and you did a public service. I don't know anything about printing a newspaper, but I do know it takes time and work."

"We're a weekly newspaper," Mr. Gordon said. "We have neither the manpower or equipment to put out a daily, but we believed the robbery and murder merited a special edition."

"I sure do appreciate your letting me read this." Lawton continued frowning at the floor and shaking his head. "There's more, though. There's got to be." Suddenly, he looked up. "This article says there were witnesses to the shooting scrape Baylor got into. Do you know who they are?"

Now Mr. Gordon was shaking his head. "No sir. We

merely took Sheriff Spates's word that there were witnesses. Fatal shootings are always news, even in Trinidad, but by the time we went to press the residents here knew all about it, and we only repeated what Sheriff Spates related to us."

"I'll bet I know where you can find out," the girl said. "If they are still in town, I'll bet you can find them at the Raton saloon. That's where the shooting took place."

"Yes," her father added, "it was just another saloon brawl. Not uncommon in this territory."

Lawton frowned at the floor again, then looked up. "Well, I'm much obliged to you both." He turned to go, but paused when the girl spoke again.

"Mr. Coop, the people here are still very, uh, angry over the bank robbery. Some of them lost all their finances. Be careful. You could be in danger."

"Thanks. I'll be careful." He went out onto the plank sidewalk.

He estimated the town's population at somewhere between six hundred and eight hundred. Still, he passed two saloons before he found the one named El Raton. The mouse. Some name. Named after the Raton Mountains, no doubt. It was a board and batten, one-story building next door to an adobe hut with a tailoring and sewing sign painted on the door. A two-acre vacant lot was on the other side, and three saddle horses stood hipshot at a hitchrail there.

Lawton paused. The door was open and black flies swarmed in and out. He could smell the whiskey clear out on the boardwalk. Finally, he stepped inside and stood there a moment, trying to accustom his eyes to the dim interior.

"Hey, New Mexico, let me buy you one."

He blinked and recognized the tall, thin O.T. cowboy he'd met at breakfast. "Sure," he said, stepping up to a long pineboard bar. "Where's your partner?"

31

The thin one grinned. "Oh, he's out fox huntin'."

Lawton knew there was a joke there somewhere, but he didn't get it. "Fox hunting?"

"Yeah, he's just gotta foxsomethin'."

Chuckling, Lawton said, "Are there foxes around here?"

"Sis Engels has got all sizes and colors. Two blocks south."

"Well, I'm a married man. I'll pass."

"Me too. They can give a man the Chinese Crud. Whiskey?" The cowboy had an empty shot glass on the bar in front of him. He was alone at the bar.

"Sounds good." Lawton took a look around, at the long plank bar, at the sandboxes for tobacco chewers spotted every ten feet on the floor, and at a half-dozen wooden tables on the other end of the room surrounded by chairs made of two-inch lumber. A big pot-bellied, wood-burning stove sat in the center of the room with a smoke pipe extending up through the ceiling. The stove was cold this time of year. Four men were playing cards at one of the tables, and a short, husky man wearing a dirty white apron stood there, watching.

"Hey, Coosie," the thin cowboy yelled, "fetch the booze."

The barkeep took his time, but eventually worked his way behind the bar. He reached under the bar for a whiskey bottle and another shot glass. Glancing at Lawton, he poured two shot glasses full, and started to put the bottle away. He glanced at Lawton again, did a double-take and took a longer look.

"You're him, ain't you." It was an accusation.

Trying to be affable, Lawton said, "Yeah, I'm him, all right, whoever he is."

"Coop, that's his name. Baylor Coop. You're his brother. I heard you was in town."

Still trying to be good-natured about it, Lawton said, "You heard already? Word travels fast."

"Yeah, I heard. What the hell're you doin' around here?"

32

The thin cowboy was looking hard at Lawton. "You're Baylor Coop's brother?"

"Yeah," Lawton said, losing his good humor. "I'm Lawton Coop, and I don't think my brother did anything wrong."

"The hell he didn't," the bartender said. "He just robbed ever' damn body around here that had any money in the bank. Hey," he yelled at the card players, "this here's Baylor Coop's brother."

"You're a kin of Baylor Coop?" The thin one couldn't believe it. "You didn't tell us that."

"I'm sure as hell not trying to hide it. Did you know my brother?"

"No. I mean, yeah, that is, I seen 'im around, that's all."

"Where did you see him?"

"In here. And out there on his homestead."

"I read in the newspaper that he was in a gunfight around here somewhere. Did you see that?"

"No. I wasn't in town then."

"Listen." Lawton took a sip of the whiskey. It had a terrible, sour, stinging taste, but he managed to keep his face straight. "I didn't come here to start any trouble. I only want to find out what happened to my brother. Would you mind telling me where his homestead is?"

Face screwed up with worry, the thin one answered, "I don't want no trouble either. I gotta go see about my horse." He dug two coins out of his pocket, slapped them onto the bar and left, walking rapidly.

Lawton watched him go and turned back to his shot glass. "Damn." He studied the glass, decided he didn't want to drink the rest of the whiskey, and looked up at the bartender. "Did you see the gunfight?"

"Yeah, I saw it. Good thing for your brother a lot of men saw it. Old Spates was lookin' for a chance to lock 'im up."

"Why? Baylor's no troublemaker."

Another voice, a deep one, came from behind Lawton.

33

"He's a goddamn double-dealing four-flushing thief."

Lawton turned his head and looked the man over. He was big, two inches taller than Lawton and weighed about thirty pounds more. A little bigger even than Baylor. He carried a six-gun in a holster low on his right hip.

"What? What did you say?" Lawton's face was red. He could feel the anger crawling into his throat.

"I said Baylor Coop is a goddamn thief. He cheated at cards and he was lucky Tip Benson's gun got caught in its cradle or he'd be deader'n rotten mutton."

The anger grew until it burst, and Lawton hissed, "That's a goddamn lie. Baylor never cheated and he never started a fight."

"You callin' me a liar?" The man was not only big, he was all muscle, and he had a square, tough face.

Anger changed to fear. Cold fear. It ran up Lawton's spine and turned his whole body cold. The man was armed. He'd left his six-gun in a cabin at the wagon yard. He could die right here. A vision of Mary flashed into his mind. Eight months pregnant. It would be stupid to die so far from home. Just plain stupid. He'd made a mistake accusing the man of lying. That wasn't the way to accomplish anything.

But, damnit, the man was lying, and he'd be damned if he'd apologize. He couldn't let the sonofabitch talk about his brother that way. The sonofabitch wanted to start a fight.

Unsure of himself, voice weak, he said, "Yeah. You're a liar."

Chapter Five

He saw the blow coming. If he hadn't been half-frozen with fear he could have sidestepped away from it. But he didn't. He just stood there with his hands down and let the big man hit him.

It caught him on the left cheek and it hurt. An explosion went off in his head and he staggered back. Another blow caught him on the side of the head and he tripped over one of the sandboxes and fell onto his back.

He intended to get up. He knew he had to get up. But his head was spinning, and the ceiling was spinning, and a church bell was ringing in his ears. He had to get up.

Another blow was coming. A big boot. A flat-heeled boot aimed at his face. He rolled, and felt it go past. Rolled and scooted back, trying to get away from the man, to get some room. The jackboots followed him. He couldn't get away. He heard someone laugh a harsh, cruel laugh. Someone said, "Stomp 'im, Ward."

Scooting back on the seat of his pants, he backed into another sandbox, saw the first one, the one he'd tripped over, at his feet. He kicked it into the big man's feet. The big man swore, stumbled over it.

His mind yelled, NOW. Now's your chance. Get up.

He scrambled to his feet, shaking his head, trying to clear

his vision, put his hands up in front of himself. The big man swung a right fist up from his knees. It was a heavy blow, but clumsy and easy to dodge. His left fist shot out, straight out from his shoulder. It smacked against the big man's right eye. He felt the shock all the way up his arm. It felt good. Another left jab and another shock. The big man was stopped.

Just stood there, shaking his head as if he couldn't believe he'd been hit that hard.

Again. And then a right cross to the jaw. The man named Ward staggered back. He was on him, throwing punches. It was good. The big man was no boxer. His right hand went numb, but it had connected with Ward's nose and the nose was spurting blood. Pour it on him. He started this fight. Give him hell.

A left hook. A right cross.

Ward was backed against the bar now, sagging against it.

Strangely, his mind recalled a yell he'd heard during a schoolyard brawl a long time ago: "Fight 'im, Law, he ain't tough, he's just ugly."

That's the way this man was. Looked tough, but easy to whip.

Another right to the jaw. Another. Ward went down. Crumpled like a sheet in the breeze.

Uh-oh. The big man's hand went to the six-gun on his hip. Move fast. Stomp on it. His boot heel crunched the big man's hand and knocked the gun away. He reached down to pick up the gun.

Another explosion went off in his head and he fell on top of Ward.

Gawd. Again he heard church bells ringing. His vision was blurred. What happened? Strong hands had him under the shoulders, lifting him. He straightened his knees, pushed back, was held.

"All right," a man's voice said, "git on your feet, Ward, and give 'im some of his own medicine."

"Wait a minute," somebody said. "This ain't fair."

"Shut yer teeth, cowboy, or you'll git the same. We ain't lettin' no sonofabitch named Coop come in here and start fights."

"He didn't start it. He . . ." Whoever was talking shut up suddenly.

"Come on, Ward. Git up."

The big man searched for his gun on the floor, found it.

"No, not that. We don't want a killin' and gittin' that lawdog on us. Just beat the cowshit out of 'im."

He tried to free himself. Kicked back, felt a boot heel connect with a shinbone. Saw Ward stand up to his full height. Saw the right-hand blow coming. Felt his face go numb. Saw another blow. Too numb now to feel it. Another. Another. Felt the hands behind him let go. Felt himself falling to the floor.

The floor felt good for a second. Only for a second. Felt a sharp pain in his right side.

Heard someone say, "All right, that's enough. We don't wanta kill 'im. Not yet, anyway."

Saw the boots leaving. Heard himself groan. Saw the ceiling swimming.

He tried to raise himself up. Fell back. Tried again. Someone was bending down, bending over him.

"I couldn't stop 'em, mister. Want some help?"

Blinking, he finally recognized the thin face of the O.T. cowboy.

"I come back when I got to thinkin' about it. I got nothin' against Baylor Coop and I got nothin' against you either. Here, let me give you a hand."

With the thin one's help he got to his feet and leaned against the bar. His head was still spinning, and the numbness was wearing off. When the numbness left, the pain arrived. Gaw-ud. His jaw ached, and his head throbbed. He

37

ran his tongue over his teeth, hoping they were still there. Found a chip in a front tooth. Spat out the chip. Tasted blood.

"A shot of whiskey might help."

"Uhnn." Lips stiff, bleeding.

"Here. Try it."

Hands trembling, he picked up the shot glass. It smelled terrible. He took a sip. It burned his throat, but helped to clear his head. Another sip, and the world stopped spinning. The next one hit his stomach like a rock, but it cleared his vision. Turning his head he saw the O.T. cowboy standing on his left. The bartender was across the bar in front of him.

"If you want, I'll help you to wherever you're stayin'," the cowboy said.

"Listen, mister." The bartender was giving him a hard scowl. "You'd better high-tail it out of these parts. Folks around here hate anybody named Coop, and the next time they'll kill you."

His strength was returning, and he straightened himself up. Stood straight. He met the bartender's scowl, and then looked around the room. The four men sat at the table, but now they weren't playing cards. They were looking at him. Ward sat there with blood on his face. Blood covered the front of his shirt.

He spoke, at first a mumble, and then with strength. "I've got only two words for the whole damn bunch of you."

They waited for him to finish.

"Go to hell is both of them."

Outside on the plank walk he inhaled deeply, and the fresh, high-altitude air was the best medicine he could have had. His legs were a little weak, but grew stronger as he walked. Wagons and buggies passed each other on Commerce Street. Pedestrians gave him curious looks as they passed. Two women stopped, turned and stared after him, their faces stern and their eyes critical. "These ruffians are always fighting," one of them said.

He walked past the Las Animas Gazette and the Trinchera Eatery, and kept going until he came to the wagon camp. There, the proprietor gave him a hard look, but took his money and said nothing. Inside the cabin, he poured water into a wash basin and splashed it over his face. He looked at himself in the mirror and groaned.

His own mother wouldn't have recognized him. One eye was swollen almost shut, a big dark bruise covered the right side of his face, and his upper lip was split and swollen and it pulled his face out of kilter.

Wouldn't Mary have a conniption if she saw him like this? She hated fighting. Said only animals fought. But she would also insist that he lie down and let her doctor him. She was good at that. She could fix him up. Wish she were here.

No, on second thought, he was glad she wasn't there.

Thinking about Mary, he tried to grin but only winced when he remembered the way she could feel the baby kicking. Their baby. Due soon.

The bed was soft, the one on springs. He let out a long sigh when he lay down. Good thing he didn't have to get up and go to work. Good to just lie here a while. He let his eyes close. He dozed.

At mid-afternoon he got up and went to look after his horses. But first, he buckled on the six-gun. Going around unarmed wasn't smart. He saddled up and rode one horse and led the other, going north where the country wasn't so steep and rocky, "legging them up," as a race horse trainer would say. Horses needed exercise. While he rode his stomach reminded him he hadn't had dinner, but he was used to skipping dinner. Did it often at home on the Circle C.

A mile out of town, on a well-worn wagon road, he saw a bunch of brick ovens, about man-high. Men worked around them. A place for making the bricks that some of the town buildings were built of.

At sundown, he went to the Trinchera Eatery, sat at the counter and ordered roast beef and mashed potatoes. He couldn't eat the beef. His jaw was too damned sore. The mashed potatoes went down easy enough, and he swallowed the bread without much chewing. The middle-aged man who'd brought him his meal noticed the problem, and said, "You ain't the first one to get his jaw busted fightin'. Want some more spuds?"

"Sure would appreciate it."

"I heard about that fight. Heard you was givin' old Ward his medicine when his pals jumped in and helped him out."

"I hope he hurts as much as I do."

"I heard your name is Coop, a brother to somebody that robbed the bank last fall."

"Do you know my brother?"

"Naw. Only just moved here a few months ago. Only just heard about him. That bread'll go down easier if you soak it in your coffee. Want some more coffee?"

"Sure do appreciate it."

While he was trying again to eat some of the beef, the two O.T. cowboys came in and occupied stools on his left. "See you're up and about," the thin one said.

Squinting at his face the short one allowed, "They sure knocked on you."

"Wish I could of stopped 'em," his partner said. "There was too many of 'em and they're bigger than me."

"Don't worry about it. I'll live." He swallowed and felt a lump in his throat. Best quit trying to eat meat. "What worries me is it didn't accomplish anything. I went there to try to find out something about my brother and didn't learn one damned thing."

The two ordered their meal. "I recognized 'im when I saw 'im, is all," the thin cowboy said. "I didn't see the shootin', only heard about it, and I heard about the poker game."

"Poker game?"

"Yeah. Way I heard it, Baylor Coop come out winner, and

40

some of the losers didn't like it and started a shootin' match. Old Baylor come out winner there too. Ain't that what you heard, Shorty?"

"Yeah. I wasn't in town either when all that happened, but that's the way I heard it."

"Tell you somebody that was here and saw it all. He don't come to town more'n a couple times a year, but he was here then and he knows, knew Baylor Coop."

Lawton stopped trying to eat, and his eyebrows went up. "Yeah? Who's that?"

"Old Willows. Weepy Willows, ever'body calls 'im cuz his eyes are always waterin'."

"Where can I find him?"

"He's got a minin' claim over south of the Picketwire, 'bout fifteen mile west and south. You got to be careful if you go to see 'im. He's got an old Henry repeatin' gun, and he don't trust nobody he don't know and he don't know very many people."

"Tell me how to find him, will you. You say he knew my brother?"

"Yeah, but you don't look much like your brother. You got to be careful."

Chapter Six

The country west of Trinidad was hilly and covered with cedars. Layers of shale cropped up everywhere and rimmed the tops of some of the hills. Lawton rode his good dun horse west, crossed the river at a wide, shallow place where the cottonwoods grew and bore south. Cedar hills surrounded him now with ravines between them. A few taller pines grew out of the cedars. Ahead, to the south, the Raton Mountains rose so high he had to tilt his head back to see the tops, and to the west was another range of mountains. Farther west he could see an even higher range, with snow in the high hollows. It was good grass country and it hadn't been grazed on that year.

The dun horse was happy to get out of the stable and walked right along, more than willing to break into a trot where the rocks weren't too numerous. A beautiful day. The sky was a clear blue, as blue as only a high-country sky can be.

Following directions laid out by the O.T. rider, he crossed a ravine and rode into a shallow canyon with walls of layered shale and a narrow creek running down the length of it. At the upper end of the canyon, he looked for the river, saw it far to the north, and reined the dun in that direction. Just before he got to it he saw four wild turkeys trying to hide in the tall grass. When he got close, two of them took to their wings and flew into a cedar. The other two ran through the grass and disappeared. Easy prey for a coyote. Easy prey for a man. Seeing a sharp bend in the river, he took a shortcut through dense scrub oak following a dim trail. The oak was as bad to ride through as the mesquite at home, and he could have used the leather leggings he usually wore.

Out of the scrubs he joined the south bank of another river, and entered another rocky canyon, this one deeper. At the top of this canyon and south of it a way he was supposed to see a one-room house made of rock with a pole roof. There was supposed to be a pole fence around two acres where the old man named Willows kept his mules.

Here was where he had to be careful. The old man could see anybody riding out of that canyon, and he didn't trust cowboys. The Maxwell bunch was always trying to run settlers off the land, and they were all cowboys. Well, no, they weren't cowboys, not according to the O.T. riders. They were hired thugs who wore cowboy clothes. A cowboy could pick another out of a crowd of gunsels at a glance, but maybe the settlers didn't know the difference.

Yet somehow, Weepy Willows had got acquainted with Baylor Coop, every inch a cowboy, and trusted him. Probably knew him better than anybody else in Las Animas County.

Grinning to himself, Lawton wished he could carry a big sign saying, "Don't Shoot. My Name Is Coop."

The grin vanished and his heart jumped into his throat when a bullet spanged off a boulder in front of him. He heard the bullet before he heard the shot. Immediately, he reined up, passed the reins under his left thigh and held up both hands.

"Don't shoot," he yelled. "I'm a friend." He looked in the direction the shot had come from, but saw nobody. "Don't shoot. My name is Coop. I'm a brother of Baylor Coop."

Another shot screamed off a rock, richocheted with a

whine out over the canyon. He had a powerful urge to turn his horse around and ride at a gallop back into the canyon. Only by strong willpower did he sit still.

Run, his mind said. Then, Don't run.

The dun was nervous over the gunshots, and he had to take hold of the reins to keep him from leaving the country. Would the next shot tear into him? If it did he wouldn't hear it. Maybe he wouldn't even feel it. An old Henry rifle, they said. Shoots .44s. Shoots fast when it works right.

"Hey, I'm a friend. Don't shoot."

He waited.

No more shots came, and that gave him hope. The shooter hadn't tried to hit him, only scare him off. He waited.

Finally, a man's voice off to his left yelled, "Come closer, but come slow. Keep your hands away from them guns. Keep your right hand up."

Reining the dun to the left, he held his free hand over his head and kept the reins snug, holding the horse to a slow walk. Ahead of him was a pile of granite boulders that looked as if the Almighty had just dropped them from the sky. He tried, squinting into the sun, but still he couldn't see anyone. The old man had to be behind one of those rocks.

"Hold up."

He reined up.

"What do'yu want?"

"I'm looking for Mr. Willows. My name is Lawton Coop. I'm a brother of Baylor Coop."

"The hell you are."

He saw him then. The man was around sixty, short, with a white beard that looked as if it had never been trimmed. His white hair was pulled back and tied in a knot at the back of his head. He stood up about fifty feet away and held the rifle to his shoulder, ready to fire again.

"Are you Mr. Willows?"

"I am. Who did you say you are?" The old man had a voice like a bellowing bull.

44

"Lawton Coop. I'm looking for my brother, Baylor Coop."

"So are a lot of folks."

"I know. I just found out about his trouble with the law. I don't think he did it."

"Well, what do'yu want from me?" Weepy Willows came out away from the boulders into the open. He wore dirty, baggy denim overalls, lace-up boots with thick soles and a red and white plaid shirt.

"I was told that you saw the shooting in Trinidad, the one where Baylor killed two men. I'd like to know all about that."

Pale blue watery eyes squinted at him, taking in the bruised and puffed face. "You don't look much like Baylor Coop."

He had to grin. "Yeah, I know. He's better looking."

The wet eyes went over him again, then, "Some folks around here got a grudge against Baylor Coop. Looks like they took it out on you."

"That's what happened, all right."

The rifle was lowered. "Git down, and come in. Got a pot of elk stew cooking. Oughta be ripe by now."

Weepy Willows turned and walked away. Lawton dismounted and followed, leading the dun. When they walked around the pile of boulders Lawton saw the house. A good stout one, built of rocks with a plank door and a steeple-shaped roof made of spruce timbers. Spruce and pine limbs had been laid tightly between the timbers and covered with dirt. And sure enough, a rock stable surrounded by a pole fence was nearby. A narrow ditch had been dug, plowed rather, through the pen, carrying water from a creek.

A team of handsome mules with collar marks stood in the pen, and a walking plow leaned against the fence. Looking around, Lawton saw no sign of plowed ground.

"Tie your horse to that old pine and come in."

He wrapped the reins around a limb of a tall pine near the

45

door, and followed the old man inside. The stew smelled good. The odor made Lawton hungry. But it was so dark in the cabin the old man had to light a lamp. There were windows, but no glass, only burlap bags to keep the flies out. Flies buzzed around inside the cabin anyway.

The furnishings consisted of a wooden bunk nailed to the far wall, a sheepherder's stove near the door, a table made of flat boards and aspen trunks, and two wooden chairs.

"Set, and we'll eat." Weepy Willows took two tin plates and two spoons from a wooden box nailed to a wall near the stove. Lawton sat in one of the chairs at the table.

"It was two riders for the O.T. outfit that told me about you. They said you knew Baylor pretty well."

"Wa-al, yes and no." Willows put the plates on the table and took the lid off an iron pot on the stove. The aroma was stronger, and it was good. "Met 'im by accident over on his claim, and we palavered a while. I was ridin' one of my jackasses. Seemed like a sociable sort. Shared a buckskin steak with me. I told 'im I was goin' to town to buy a few vittles, and he 'lowed he'd go along. Never did get real well acquainted with him, howsomever."

"Did you see the gunfight?"

With a ladle, Willows filled the tin plates, sat and picked up a spoon. "Yup, I did. Wasn't that boy's fault. They put 'im in a spot where he had to fight or run. That's what I told that sorry excuse for a sheriff they had around here then."

As hungry as he was, and as good as the stew smelled, Lawton was too curious to eat. "Would you tell me what happened?"

"Eat, and then we'll talk."

He experimented with a small bite of meat. It was delicious. He'd eaten venison before, but not elk meat. It was cut up in small chunks and stewed with potatoes, carrots, turnips, and enough water to make a thick gravy. Tasty, and tender enough that he could chew it in spite of a sore jaw. Carefully. The old man didn't look up again until he'd cleaned his plate. Then he tilted his chair back on its hind legs and pulled a corncob pipe out of a shirt pocket.

"Generally have some biscuits, but I ran out of flour. Gonna have to take a trip to town purty soon." He filled the pipe from a cotton sack of tobacco and lit up.

"That was the best stew I ever threw a lip over," Lawton allowed. "Elk, you said?"

"Yeah, shot a young bull last week. Nothing better'n elk."

"Bet a man could live pretty cheap around here, with all this wild meat running around."

"Some folks do. Have to buy a few vittles, howsomever."

"I saw some turkeys coming up here. Ever eat one?"

"You betcha. Good eatin'. Care for a smoke?"

"Naw. Never got the habit."

"A chaw?"

"Huh-uh. Thanks just the same."

"Your brother liked a chaw now and then."

"He did? Wonder when he picked up that habit."

The old man snorted and slapped the table with an open hand. "Just testin' you, son. That boy didn't smoke or chew either."

"If you have any doubts, I can tell you all about him."

"None a-tall. You talk like 'im and when I look close I can see the family resemblance. It's in the eyes and jaw. And you got good manners, like he did."

"You talk about him as if he was dead."

"Naw. He ain't dead. He's as tough as they come. When he has to be."

"Do you know where he is?"

Two puffs of smoke came from between the old man's lips before he answered, "Naw. He could be a long way from here. If I was in his boots I'd shore put a lot of country between me and this territory."

"They're accusing him of murder and robbery. Do you think he did it?"

The wet eyes looked sad, and the old man shook his head.

47

"I don't know, son. I wouldn't a trusted that sheriff no farther than I could a throwed 'im up the side of that hill over there, but I just plain don't know what happened."

They were silent a moment. Lawton was trying to picture Baylor robbing a bank, and couldn't. Weepy Willows smoked his pipe, then, "It's civilization that done it."

"Huh?"

"Laws and lawmen. Many a good man has turned bad when they tried to slap too many laws on 'em."

Willows seemed to want to say more, and Lawton kept quiet.

"Happens ever' time. They wanta git civilized, and they elect a gover'ment and they elect a sheriff, and they start orderin' people around. Some people don't take to it."

Lawton didn't know what to say to that so he remained silent.

"It's do this and do that or else they'll throw you in jail, by God. Hell, some men just won't allow it."

"Well, uh, Baylor believed in law and order."

"Shore, he did. And look what it got 'im. Where was the goddamn laws when them two jumped 'im in that El Raton Saloon? If he'd a been one a them book thumpin' civilized men and left his six-gun at home, he'd be dead. Shot full of holes. And I'll bet the goddamn laws wouldn't a done nothin' about it."

"Well, uh, they would have arrested the men who shot him."

"Shore, and what good would that a done your brother? He'd a been dead, wouldn't he? Laws or no laws."

All Lawton could do was shake his head in agreement.

"Next thing you know they'll be puttin' a tax on us. Folks that ain't go two nickels to rub together'll have to pay the goddamn gover'ment."

The more the old man talked, the faster he puffed his pipe, and Lawton could see he was making himself angry. He tried

48

to change the subject. "Uh, Mr. Willows, will you tell me about that gunfight?"

"Know why my eyes're always waterin'? Cuz I got a allergy, that's why? Know what I'm allergic to? Civilization, that's what. That's why I stay up here. If you think my old peepers're wet now, you ought to see 'em when I go to town. Hell, I can't hardly see through 'em."

"Did you see what happened in that gunfight?"

"Shore, I saw it. We only just got to town. Tied our animals in that trap next to the saloon and went in to have a sociable drink of whiskey."

"What happened?"

"They braced 'im. We no more'n got in the door when those two birds came up and ask that boy if he wanted to play some poker. He said no, he didn't have any money. They didn't believe 'im, said he oughta give 'em a chance to win their money back, and called 'im a liar."

"Ohhh," Lawton groaned. "Where we came from, you don't call a man a liar unless you want a fight."

"Not where I come from either, nor anywhere I've been. Them two wanted to kill that boy. But he was too fast for 'em. One of 'em, the biggest of the two, pulled his six-shooter and let 'er rip."

"What? How . . . ?"

"But he was dead on his feet, and his slug hit the floor. That boy whipped out his six-gun so fast I didn't even see 'im do it, and he drilled that ranihan right through the chest."

"But the other one, what . . . ?"

"That other jasper was dumb. My jackasses've got better sense than he did. He saw how fast that boy could draw and shoot, and still he had the plain stupidity to grab for his gun. Hell, he was dead before he got it halfway out of his holster."

"Huh." Lawton let the air out of his lungs with a grunt. "Baylor can shoot. No doubt about that. What did the sheriff do? Anything at all?"

"Wasn't nothin' he could do. Lots of men saw what happened, and told about it. Had a coroner's in . . . uh . . ."

"Inquest?"

"And they ruled that boy was only defendin' hisself."

"There's a coroner in Trinidad, huh?"

"A doctor. Says he's a doctor."

Lawton was silent a moment as he digested that.

"There was somethin' that law dog said, though, that has kinda stuck in my mind."

"What?"

"He said that boy was gonna git hisself in a lot of trouble. In fact, he said he'd guarantee it."

Chapter Seven

Weepy Willows didn't know much about Baylor Coop. Never asked him where he was from, didn't believe in asking a man too many questions.

Outside, in the shade of a tall spruce where the flies weren't so bad, he squatted on his heels and told of visiting Baylor twice at Baylor's claim. The first time was an accident. He came upon the young man before he realized anyone was there, and he didn't know whether to wave a friendly greeting or be ready to fight. But the young cowboy had waved him over and shared a pot of coffee with him. Baylor had a one-room cabin built, and a corral where he kept two horses. He was one of many who had picked out a piece of land and built a shelter, believing the Right of Discovery made it theirs. After all, the land belonged to the people and the people had a right to use it. Willows said Baylor talked about buying some cattle somewhere and raising a few calves.

Lawton asked about the Maxwell Company, and Willows repeated what the two O.T. cowboys had said, that the company claimed the land was not public domain, and ran the squatters off, trading shots with some of them, and killing at least two.

"I heard that the United States Congress ruled the land

51

does belong to the Maxwell," Lawton said.

"That's the way they tell it, but they ain't proved it to me. That sheriff came up here once and told me I'd have to git, and I ran 'im off. Some of them Denver ranihans the Maxwell hired tried to sneak up on me one day, but I plugged one of them in the laig, and they never came back. They will, howsomever. They'll be back."

"What will you do? You can't fight them off forever."

"See that hill over there?" Willows pointed with a callused finger to the side of a high ridge about a hundred yards away. "I got a shaft dug in 'er, and I take enough color out of 'er to buy me what little I need. You can't see 'er from here. I got 'er hid. But she's there, and she's been good to me, and I ain't givin' 'er up."

Not knowing what to say, Lawton just shook his head.

"They might berry me here, but right here's where I stay."

Still shaking his head, Lawton stared at the ground between his boots. It was a sad story. The old man had wandered around the country, and finally found what he wanted, a vein of gold and the materials to build a cabin. He had worked hard, and he still worked hard, but he liked the isolation and he liked the independence. Now, the government has ruled that the land belongs to somebody else. Somebody else will profit from his labors.

Lawton glanced at the old man, then looked at the ground again. "I'm a cowman, Mr. Willows, and cows need a hell of a lot of territory, especially in the Pecos Valley." He continued looking down, feeling a need to explain his beliefs. "My granddad and my dad were the first to use the land. There wasn't a settlement for over a hundred miles, and they lived a hard life, a very hard life. They fought the Apaches, and they fought the rustlers. My granddad died when he was dragged by a horse, and my dad was killed by the 'Paches. Other cattlemen recognized their rights, even though it was unwritten, and there was no trouble. And then somebody started a stageline and built a relay station on their land and built a store. My folks liked having a store there and they didn't complain. But when the stage road was built and the store was built, the sodbusters started moving in. Then there was trouble."

They were silent, and Lawton realized he'd talked more than he was accustomed to. But he had to finish saying what was on his mind. "It's hard to tell folks where they can settle and where they can't. But when you see some of your stock dead from dehydration because the farmers have fenced off the water, you can't help being fighting mad. The farmers can run a cowman out of business in a hurry. However." He looked over at the old man. Willows was staring at the ground too. "If you had this on my land, I'd say you were entitled to it."

He stood, and Willows stood too and stretched his legs. Lawton held out his hand to shake. The old man shook with him.

"All I can say, Mr. Willows, is I wish you the best of luck. I hope you live a long and happy life."

"I'll tell you this, young feller, I'm kinda glad I'm gettin' old. The way folks are leavin' the east and comin' west, in another fifty years there ain't gonna be standin' room." With that, Weepy Willows turned on his heels and went into his cabin.

Lawton untied the dun, tightened the cinches and mounted. He looked back once, then rode away toward the canyon.

A buck deer with a wide rack of antlers ran across an acre-sized vega at the bottom of the canyon. It ran as a rubber ball bounces, not very much afraid of the man on a horse, but not taking any chances. Baylor's claim, what he'd called his claim, wasn't far from here. Lawton had ridden within a mile of it earlier that day without knowing it. He turned his horse south and went looking for it.

Wishing now he hadn't stayed so long at Old Man Willows's place, Lawton doubted he'd have time to look over the spot where his brother had once settled and get back to town before dark. His horse was a stranger in these parts too and wouldn't know the way back. With a sudden change of mind, he turned the horse again and headed for town. He didn't want to get lost in the dark.

As he rode, his mind was heavy, thinking about Weepy Willows, his brother's claim and the others who'd settled on the Maxwell. He was sorry for them, yet he couldn't entirely blame the Maxwells either. If it was legally theirs, it was theirs and that was that.

His granddad and his dad didn't always agree with the law, but they'd tried to abide by it. They'd staked out what they estimated to be a hundred thousand acres, and drove two thousand longhorn cattle from Texas. No one else was using the land. The buffalo were mostly gone, and the Apache were mostly gone too. Only a handful of braves came around now and then to steal what they could and take what white men's scalps they could. The Apaches helped themselves to Circle C beef, and there was little anyone could do about it.

Then, years later, when the land was finally surveyed, the Coops took advantage of the old U.S. Preemption Law, and bought the land from the government. They'd had trouble with squatters, but not much. The land was no good for farming, and the squatters soon discovered that. There were a half-dozen rickety old shacks on the Circle C where the land had been plowed up and farmers had lived, trying to raise crops. Only the shacks were there now, and weeds where grass once grew.

Baylor Coop was a cattleman, and his brother Lawton couldn't understand why he'd tried to move in on somebody else's land. There was more to this than he'd been told. Baylor Coop was no squatter.

His horses fed, he walked to the Trinchera Eatery to feed

himself. His jaw was still sore, but getting better. He managed to get enough food chewed and swallowed to prevent any hunger pangs. Back at the wagon camp, he was walking to his cabin when the manager hailed him.

"Got a note for you. Here." He handed him an envelope with the name "Mr. Lawton Coop" written on it in ink.

"Thanks," he said.

Inside the cabin, he lit a lamp and opened the envelope. It contained a single sheet of paper with a short message:

"Mr. Coop, please come into the Gazette office tomorrow morning. I would like to talk to you about your brother, Baylor Coop." It was signed Annie Gordon.

Fine. He'd already decided he wanted to talk to that girl again. Something she'd said was sticking in his mind. She'd said Baylor told her he'd bought some land. Six hundred acres. Bought it, not squatted on it. This was something he'd have to learn more about.

She was alone in the building, as pretty as she was the first time he'd seen her, with her dark brown hair, dark sparkling eyes and that small dimple in her chin. She smiled a pretty smile when he came through the door, and he couldn't help smiling with her.

"Good morning, Mr. Coop. Thank you for coming."

"Morning, Miss Gordon. I was glad to get your note. I wanted to see you again anyway."

"Please be seated." She sat on a high wooden stool and waved him to the desk chair. "I, uh, don't really know what to say, Mr. Coop, except that I knew Baylor better than I've let on. He visited me several times."

Lawton was quiet, letting her say what she wanted to say without interruption.

"We were not, uh, close, but I did know him. I . . ." Her eyes were downcast. Then she looked up, looked at him squarely, and added, "The more I think about it, the more

I'm convinced that Baylor is no thief nor murderer."

"What makes you think that, Miss Gordon?"

"He's just not that sort. I mean, you can't always tell about a man, but I just don't believe it." She was silent a moment, looking down again, then, "When he shot those two men at El Raton, I told myself to keep away from him. I thought he was a saloon brawler. But . . . Mr. Coop, we, my father and I, came here from a small town in Illinoi, and everything here is different. I mean, I've come to realize that here there is very little law, and a man sometimes has to defend himself. I heard about your fight too, and how it started. I . . ."

When she paused, he said, "Baylor never ran from a fight, but I don't believe he ever started a fight either. I talked with a gentleman name of Willows yesterday and he saw the whole thing and said Baylor had to kill or be killed. It does happen that way sometimes."

"Yes, I know that now. I eventually allowed Baylor to visit me again at our home, and while he is not what you could call a refined gentleman, he's no hoodlum either."

"Do you know where Baylor is?"

She shook her head. "No, I honestly do not. I can only hope that he is all right."

"Would you mind telling me, when did you see him last?"

"The night of the robbery and murder. He had been gone for a time, after he broke out of jail, and he suddenly showed up at our house that night and called me outside. He, uh, said he was leaving and wanted to say goodbye."

"That was all he said?"

"Yes. He was rather mysterious, very mysterious, and would say no more."

"Hmm." He studied the floor. "Well. Hmm. Oh." He looked up. "Did I understand you to say Baylor had bought some land?"

"Yes. That's what he said. He had plans. He was going into the cattle business."

"And it was on the Maxwell?"

"Yes, but he said he bought it and there was to be no trouble over it."

"Well." He stood. "If he bought it he had a deed to it, and the deed should be recorded with the county clerk."

"Yes, I believe so."

"Is that the courthouse, that new building?"

"Yes it is, and the county clerk has an office there."

"That, then, is where I'm going next. Thanks a lot, Miss Gordon."

"Call me Annie, please."

"All right. That is, if you'll call me Lawton. Or Law."

"Sure. Uh, Mr., uh Lawton, I probably shouldn't say this, but I haven't been able to get Baylor out of my mind. I tried, but . . . if you see him, or if you communicate with him, would you tell him something for me?"

"You betcha."

"Tell him that . . . well, just tell him that I'm on his side."

"He's a lucky man, Annie. He'll be real happy to know that."

Chapter Eight

It was a brick and rock building. Except for the two-story hotel it was the biggest building in town, covering over fifteen hundred square feet. Inside, the thick walls and high ceiling kept it cool, despite the heat outside. His boots thumped on the wooden floor as he walked down a narrow hall, looking for the county clerk's office. The floor had been made of new lumber, and it had shrunk a little, leaving cracks between the floorboards. The whole building smelled new.

He walked past a courtroom with two rows of planks for seats, a high judge's bench and a chair behind it. The room was empty. The next door had a sign painted on it: "La Animas County Clerk." He opened a wooden door on steel hinges and went in.

It was a small room, with a wooden cabinet full of pull-out drawers and a short counter. Only one person occupied the room, and she was seated at a new desk behind the counter. Another sign propped on her desk said, "Mrs. Margaret Tuders, County Clerk."

"Excuse me," Lawton said, "Are you Mrs. Tuders?"

Looking up, she answered pleasantly, "Yes, I am. What can I do for you?" She was middle-aged, plump. Her hair was streaked with gray.

"I, uh, I'd like to check on something. A gentleman named Baylor Coop said he bought six hundred acres of land in this county, and I wonder if a deed to that land has been recorded."

She was shaking her head before he finished talking. "No sir. There is no record of that."

"You know without looking?"

"Yes sir." She stood in her long cotton dress and came over to the counter. "I've looked and looked. Mr. Coop himself asked about it."

"How long ago was that?"

"It was last summer. Late summer. I disremember the exact date."

"Baylor Coop himself? Isn't that strange? I mean why would he ask about it if he saw it recorded? He did see it recorded, didn't he?"

"He said he did, but there is no deed on file here."

"But . . ." Lawton's mind raced, trying to figure it out. "How could that be?"

She shrugged, and her features pulled together. "I can only guess. He had a deed in his hand. I mean he had what appeared to be a deed. But it could have been a fake. We figure the land was sold to him by one of those land swindlers in Denver, and the deed he had in his hand was worthless. Or . . ." Her voice trailed off.

"Or what?"

"Well, in light of what happened later, I mean the bank robbery and the murder of Sheriff Spates, we figure he was just trying to lay claim to some land he never had any right to."

"No, ma'am. Not Baylor Coop."

She was squinting at him now. "You're not . . . you're his brother, aren't you? I heard his brother was in town. And you've been fighting."

"Yes, ma'am, I am. My name is Lawton Coop. I'm here to find out what happened to my brother."

Her face hardened. "Well, I've told you everything I can. There is no land deed here with his name on it, and there is no record of that land he claimed ever having been sold."

He realized he was staring at her with a disbelieving expression on his face, but he couldn't help it. "Does that land belong to the Maxwell Land Company?"

"I believe it does. However, since I have no description of it I can't be sure."

"Hmm. Well, thank you for your time." He turned to go, stopped and looked back. "Tell me, are you the only one responsible for recording land transactions?"

"Yes, that's correct."

"Then, if Baylor Coop came in here and asked that a land transaction be recorded, you would know about it?"

"Yes, that's, uh, maybe not."

"What do you mean, Mrs. Tuders?" He turned back, facing her again.

"Mr. Jackson, Orville Jackson, was county clerk at the time the transaction had supposedly taken place."

"Oh?" Lawton's eyebrows went up. "Did anybody ask him about it?"

"No sir. Mr. Jackson passed away last summer. Or fall."

"He did?" This was interesting.

"Yes. He was a lunger. He died of the consumption. We all knew he didn't have long to live."

"Could he have . . . ?"

Shaking her head again, she said, "No. He kept records of everything. He was an excellent clerk. Even when he packed to move into this building everything was in proper order. There was no record of a land transaction involving Baylor Coop."

"And now he's dead." He said it as a statement, not as a question.

"He died in his sleep."

Lawton's shoulders slumped. Again he turned to go. "Well, thanks again, Mrs. Tuders."

"You seem like a nice young man."

Again, he looked back. "Listen, Mrs. Tuders, my brother Baylor is a nice young man, too. Maybe he doesn't have the manners of the city slicks, but he's honest and I don't believe he did everything he's accused of."

"He did seem sincere, but . . . he was recognized. There is no mistake."

"And you think he was the victim of some swindler?"

"That's the only explanation. Lots of people come to this territory looking for free land. There is free land, but not over there where Mr. Coop said he bought land. The United States Congress has ruled that it belongs to the Maxwells. All one-and-a-half-million acres of it."

"A million and a half acres."

"That's the best estimate. It has been surveyed by the United States Government. Most of it is in the New Mexico Territory. The swindlers have sold fake titles to people for fifty cents an acre."

"What does most land sell for in this territory?"

"Those who would rather buy it from the government than prove up on it pay a dollar and twenty-five cents an acre. And at that, they can buy only in certain areas."

A grim smile touched his lips. "That makes the Maxwell land look pretty good at fifty cents."

She shrugged again. "The swindlers are very busy. But there is nothing we can do about it."

"Did Baylor say who he bought the land from?"

"Of course. He . . ." She paused, thinking. "He had to have mentioned it to Mr. Jackson and Sheriff Spates."

"But not to you?"

"No sir."

"He did see Orville Jackson about it then?"

"I believe he did. He came here and asked me to look up the record, and when I couldn't find it he said he was going to Mr. Jackson's house. Mr. Jackson was very ill."

"Uh-huh." Lawton considered that. "Then the only ones

who knew who he bought the land from were the county clerk and the sheriff, and they're both dead. And the man he bought it from." He added sarcastically, "I hope he's still alive."

"That's all I can tell you, sir."

"Thanks again."

The bright sun struck him full in the face as he stepped into the heat of Commerce Street, and he pulled his hat brim down to ward it off. Baylor Coop had been involved in the sale, purchase and trade of land before. He knew what he was doing. He'd been swindled, all right.

But not by anyone from Denver.

The sun was near its peak in the sky, and he figured he wouldn't have time to ride out to Baylor's claim, look it over and get back before dark. Still, he couldn't just kill time. He wondered if he could get any more information out of Sheriff Horace Willard. Somebody had said he was "all right." That meant he was honest, if nothing else. He decided to try, and stomped his way along the boardwalk to the sheriff's office and jail. Not there. Hell.

As he turned to leave, he saw the sheriff coming on foot from the opposite direction, his wide-brim hat pulled low, the silver star on his shirt glinting in the sun. When he came close, he squinted at Lawton.

"Got yourself beat up already, huh? Heard about that brawl. Do that again, and I'll have to lock you up. Folks around here are getting damned tired of fighting and shooting."

"It wasn't my idea, Sheriff. I didn't come here to fight anybody."

"That's why you're not in the pokey. I done gave you the benefit of the doubt."

"Yeah, well." He didn't much like the attitude of the sheriff, but he wanted information from him, and he tried to be civil. "I'd like to talk to you a minute if you've got time."

"Come in." Sheriff Willard opened the door, went in and plopped down in his desk chair. Lawton sat in the other chair.

"Did you know Sheriff Spates very well?"

"Didn't have much traffic with him, no. Why?" The sheriff lifted his hat and scratched his nearly bald head, reset his hat.

Lawton shrugged. "There's something strange. My brother said he bought some land from the Maxwell, yet there's no record of it."

"Who'd he say that to?"

"Why, uh . . ." No, by damn, he wasn't going to get Annie Gordon mixed up in this. "He went to the county clerk's office and tried to find a record of it. If he hadn't bought it he wouldn't have done that."

"Oh, he prob'ly bought it, all right, but not from the rightful owners. Prob'ly from some grifter from Denver."

"Huh-uh. He's a cattleman. Our family owns a hundred thousand acres in southern New Mexico. He wouldn't be easy to swindle."

"Wa-al, there's no record of a land sale in his name, and that deed he had was forged, and that's that."

"Did he tell you who he bought it from?"

"Not me. But you understand I wasn't sheriff then. I got a few cows and a few sections of my own east of town a ways, and back then I had no idea of being a lawman."

"Did you ever hear of him naming the man he bought the land from?"

"Nope. Can't say that I have."

"I've been told the Maxwell Company is selling land."

"Sure. They'll sell to them that can pay. That's why they bought out the Maxwell family, to sell land. Hell, they can't use a million and a half acres."

"Hmm." Lawton studied the floor. It needed sweeping. He looked up. "Has anybody else complained about buying land and not having it recorded with the county?"

"Nope. Not that I've heard of."

"So they're offering land for sale. Do they intend to sell the whole grant?"

"No. They're running some cattle over there, and there's some land they won't sell."

"Hmm. Well, how about the settlers? The people who settled there before the U.S. Government gave it to the Maxwells? Are they buying land?"

"Some of them are. In fact, the company is being right generous with them. Giving them several years to pay for it, as long as they pay something now to show good faith."

"Well, I've been told that they're running settlers off. In fact, I've been told there's been some shooting and some men killed."

The sheriff shook his head sadly. "They've got a right to protect their property. If you found squatters on your land, what would you do?"

"Get the sheriff to run them off."

Another negative shake of the head. "I prob'ly won't be sheriff beyond the next election, but I just ain't got the heart to go shoot at people who've been working the land for years and don't want to leave. I went to them and told them what the law is, and I can only hope they work out a deal with the company. My dad homesteaded, and I homesteaded, and nobody's going to tell me to git."

Silently, Lawton sympathized with the sheriff. He couldn't do it either. But he wondered why Horace Willard wanted to be sheriff. Willard answered that question without being asked.

"After Bill Spates was murdered, some of the folks around here practically begged me to run for election. A lot of folks. Mostly, folks that've been in these parts for a long time. I just got talked into it. I won't run again."

Lawton was silent a moment. He could understand. Here was a man who was supposed to use gunfire if necessary to run people out of their homes, people he might have known most of his life. If that was what lawmen had to do, then nobody with any self-respect would be a lawman. Well, this wasn't getting him anywhere.

"Uh, Mr. Willard, my brother is accused of jailbreak, among other things. Do you know why he was in jail?"

"Way I heard it, he wouldn't get off that piece of ground he claimed. Sheriff Spates locked him up to discourage him from going back."

Lawton couldn't believe it. No sir. If Baylor thought he had a right to that land he'd fight for it. The only way they could have got him off was to carry him off. But he asked no more questions about that.

"Does the Maxwell Company have a land office, or anything?"

"Only at the bank. Ben Mock is managing the land company and he's chief stockholder at the bank. He's got an office there."

"Mock," Lawton repeated. "Isn't he the one my brother was supposed to have robbed?"

"He's the one. And if I was you, young feller, I wouldn't go up to him and introduce myself."

"Yeah, well . . ." Lawton shrugged.

Outside, on the sidewalk, pedestrian traffic was heavy. Women wore wool shawls around their shoulders despite the heat, and the men wore overalls and jackboots. Mexicans wore their straw sombreros and sandals, and kids were in ragged cotton pants and went barefoot. As wagons rumbled by, the horses snorted at the sights and sounds of the town.

The sheriff's advice was good. Benjamin Mock wouldn't be friendly with anyone named Coop. But Lawton wanted to meet the man.

Yep. The more he thought about it, that was one gentleman he damned sure wanted to meet.

Chapter Nine

Surprise. Benjamin Mock greeted him cordially. "I heard you were in town," he said, standing up behind a big mahogany desk. "Please have a seat." He waved toward a comfortable-looking padded armchair in front of the desk. "Cigar?"

"No thanks," Lawton said. "I never got the habit." He sat, held his hat in his lap and crossed his legs.

"I understand you're looking for your brother, Baylor Coop." Benjamin Mock chuckled. "You understand, of course, that lawmen all over the country are also looking for him." He was about Lawton's height, a little heavier, smooth-faced, also average-looking.

Getting in to see Mr. Mock had been no trouble at all. A pretty girl at a smaller desk in the bank lobby had led him to a closed door on the far side of a low wrought-iron fence. The fence separated the public from the inner sanctum. She had even opened the gate for him. "May I ask who is calling?" Then she preceded him into the office. He went in when she came out.

"You should understand too, Mr. Mock, that the Coop family is a respected ranching family in southern New Mexico Territory. It's hard for me to believe my brother is guilty of anything dishonest."

"Yes, I could tell he was a cattleman, and not the usual sort of grifter and hoodlum we often have to deal with."

Lawton uncrossed his legs, recrossed them. "I understand he bought some land on the Maxwell grant."

The smile stayed on Benjamin Mock's face, but he shook his head. "No. Unfortunately, he thought he bought some land, but I'm afraid he was duped. It has happened so many times. Ever since Congress ruled that the land does not belong to the United States government, grifters have sold fake deeds to land there."

Lawton considered arguing the point, but decided it would be useless. "Are you selling land on the grant?"

"Of course. It is a very large investment. The Maxwell Land Company expects to make a profit."

"How about the settlers who were there before Congress got into it? What are you doing about them?"

The smile widened. "We're getting into something rather, uh, personal here, Mr. Coop, but I understand your curiosity. I'll tell you this, we have worked out a plan with most of the settlers that is satisfactory to both sides. They have an option to buy the land they want. If they can't pay immediately, we will give them five years to pay. Of course, we have to have some faith money. Not much, just enough to show good faith."

The smile was not returned. Lawton didn't feel like smiling. He studied Benjamin Mock's face, trying to find fault with the man. The face was good-natured and sincere.

"Those who choose to buy are given a deed and the deeds are recorded. But with a cloud on the title. The cloud is removed when the purchase price is paid in full. Everything is open and above board."

"I've been told that some settlers are refusing to pay and refusing to move."

Finally, the smile slipped. "Yes. That is very unfortunate." The smile was back. "What would you do, Mr. Coop, if you were in our boots?"

He couldn't meet the man's gaze, and he looked down. "I'll have to admit, we've had that problem. Only, the settlers on our land hadn't been there long, and they wouldn't have stayed anyhow."

"But you see what our problem is."

"Yeah." He had to admit it.

"Mr. Coop." Benjamin Mock leaned forward and put his elbows on the desk. The smile was gone, but there was no animosity. "Baylor Coop put a gun to my head and forced me to open the bank's safe. When Sheriff Spates came to see what was happening, Baylor Coop shot him dead. Now, you seem to be a pretty intelligent and decent sort of man, and I'm sorry it was your brother who committed those crimes. And I believe you when you say you know nothing of your brother's whereabouts. But if I were you, I would just go on back to New Mexico Territory and try to forget you have a brother."

Lawton uncrossed his legs and planted both feet on the floor. "Is that a threat?"

"No. Of course not. It's just friendly advice. I have every reason to want to shoot Baylor Coop on sight, but I'm not taking it out on his brother. However, it is obvious that someone did take it out on you. There are others who are more vicious than I."

"Yeah, well." He stood. "Thank you for your time, Mr. Mock."

He was glad to see potato soup on the handwritten menu at the Trinchera Eatery. Not as filling as meat, but a hell of a lot easier to chew.

"Seen those two riders for the O.T. today?" he asked the man behind the counter.

"I think they dusted out of here. Went back to O.T. headquarters. Prob'ly shot their wad in El Raton and the cathouse."

He had to blow on the soup to cool it, and while he ate, he thought over his conversation with Benjamin Mock. A gentleman. Pleasant. Good-natured. Seemed to be honest. Try as he did, Lawton could find no flaw in the man's character. The bankers he'd known were honest men who made it possible for a cattleman to go into business. Or stay in business. The Circle C wouldn't be big enough to support two families if the Coops hadn't been able to borrow money to buy land and cattle. Bankers took a chance, lending money. They couldn't be blamed for trying to make a profit.

And the Maxwell Land Company? A bunch of investors who expected to sell the Maxwell grant in small pieces and get more money than they paid. Couldn't hold that against them. They were doing the best they could in dealing with the settlers. Hell, they couldn't just give the land away.

He wiped his soup bowl clean with a piece of bread and ate the bread. His jaw was healing.

And if they were selling land, there was no reason they wouldn't sell to Baylor Coop. Could it be that Baylor did get duped? Or did he just try to put something over on somebody?

Naw.

Outside, the sky was cloudy. He looked up. Where did those clouds come from? Clear as a church bell an hour ago. Strange climate. Cloudy and cool.

His horses were snorty when he led them out of the stable and saddled the dun. Lightning streaked the sky to the west. Thunder boomed. He rode north at a trot, hoping to leg the horses up before the rain came. It didn't work out that way. He was four miles from town, riding at a lope, leading the bay packhorse, when the first drops fell. Cold.

Damn. Rain was such a welcome sight in the Pecos Valley that he never carried a slicker. Rain there was warm and pleasant. Not up here. Cold enough to freeze the cods off a brass monkey. He turned around and headed back on a gallop. But a mile from town, he pulled the horses down to a walk. Best have them cooled off when he put them back in the stable. A horse that's quiet and calm when he's unsaddled is more likely to be quiet and calm when he's caught again.

By the time he got back to the rented cabin, he was soaked. There was a one-lid cookstove, but no firewood, so he stripped and wrapped himself in a blanket. Grinning inwardly, he wished he'd had a bar of soap while he was out there. He could use a bath.

While he sat on the edge of the bed getting warm, he went over in his mind what he'd learned since coming to Trinidad. Nothing good. Baylor was wanted for robbery and murder. He'd bought a piece of land, or thought he did, but couldn't prove it. He was arrested and thrown in jail because he refused to give up the land. He broke out of jail somehow and disappeared for a while, then came back one night. That was the last that anyone around here had seen of him. So they said.

All right, so where did he get the money to buy the land? When he left home he was heading for the gold fields around Pikes Peak. He admitted in his last letter that he hadn't found any gold, and was working his way south, just to see the country. He hadn't stayed long in Pueblo, that was obvious. He'd come on south to Trinidad. Then what?

There was a poker game. He must have won. The gunfight broke out because he wouldn't give the losers a chance to win it back. Told them he didn't have it.

Uh-huh. That's where he got enough money to buy some land. Won it in a poker game. Must have been some game. Lawton would like to know about that. Who could tell him? Some of the men who hung around El Raton?

Grinning at himself again, Lawton shook his head. No sir. He wasn't going back in there.

But on second thought, if he was going to find out anything, he had to ask. Yeah, he'd go back.

Only, next time he'd carry a gun.

* * *

No use waiting. The best time to go to a saloon was in the evening when it would be crowded. Get some supper and go. He got dressed in one of two changes of clothes he'd brought and buckled on the six-gun. At first, he drew the gunbelt tight enough to hold the gun high on his right hip where it was out of the way when he mounted or dismounted a horse. But then he let the belt out a notch, allowing the holstered gun to hang lower, closer to his hand.

A gunfighter's position.

He was right. El Raton was crowded. Two bartenders were working as fast as they could, pouring whiskey, making change from cigar boxes under the bar. He stepped up and ordered whiskey. The bartender was the one who was working the day he got beat up. He did a double-take, but said nothing.

Lawton sipped the whiskey. Rotgut. Forcing himself to keep his face straight, he turned his back to the bar and looked over the room. Must have been twenty-five customers, all men. Nearly all carrying six-guns. Three of the gaming tables were occupied and cards were being shuffled and dealt. Money was changing hands.

"Say, ain't you . . . yeah, you're him."

Lawton looked to his left. The man who spoke was short and wide with a week's growth of whiskers on a tough face.

"Didn't you get enough the last time?" He wore a floppy black hat and boots with flat heels.

Lawton half-turned and faced the man, "I'm looking for information, not trouble."

"Shit, mister, you are trouble. That goddamn brother of yours cleaned out the bank and cleaned out a lot of people. Best thing you can do is haul your ass out of here."

Shaking his head, Lawton said, "I only want to find out exactly what happened. I don't think my brother is guilty of stealing."

"Shit, two people recognized 'im."

This was getting nowhere. Lawton tried to change the subject. "I heard my brother won some money in a poker

71

game. Would you happen to know anything about that?"

Before the short man could answer, another gent stepped up. "What the hell're you doin' back in here? Get your ass out before you git carried out."

Lawton recognized him. He was one of the toughs who had held him while another tough beat on him. Seeing him brought an angry bile to Lawton's throat. Turning so he could face both men, he said, "If I'm carried out, you can bet your ass and all its fixtures you'll go out ahead of me."

"Oh, you're packing iron now, are you." The man sneered, "We got ways of takin' care of you Coops."

Sneering himself, Lawton said, "You didn't do so good with Baylor Coop."

"Sic 'im, Heavy." This was still another voice. Another man. On Lawton's right. Now there was a man on each side of him and one in front. Damn.

Keeping his eyes on the tough named Heavy, Lawton stepped back one step and got his back against the bar. He stood with his feet apart, his right hand hanging down, fingers close to the Colt. "I didn't come in here to fight. I only wanted to find out about a poker game my brother was in. But I'll tell you one thing, if I get shot, at least one of you is gonna get it first."

"There's three of us. Go ahead and draw."

"You'll be the first to die," Lawton said, looking straight at Heavy. "If either one of your pals makes a move, you'll die." His heart was beating too fast, and his guts were twisting into a knot, but he forced himself to stand straight and keep the fear out of his face.

It was suddenly quiet in El Raton. A crowd had gathered, their eyes going from one man to another, their mouths closed.

"You think you can take all of us?" Heavy said.

"No, but I'll get you." His eyes didn't move from Heavy's face. "Go ahead, reach for your guns. Any of you. And this big sonofabitch will die right there."

No one moved. Except Heavy. And he moved only his eyes, trying to take in the crowd.

"This here's Baylor Coop's brother. Just as big a thief as he is. We can't let 'im walk out of here."

Still, no one moved.

Lawton's guts were knotted and his hands wanted to tremble. He couldn't let that happen. He willed his body to be strong.

Through his teeth, he said, "Draw or git."

Their eyes were locked now. No sound at all, except the breathing of the crowd.

Lawton didn't know how long he could stand it. His knees wanted to tremble and his heart was beating like an Apache war drum. Now he wanted Heavy to move. Wanted something to happen. Something had to happen.

Finally, someone did move. But it wasn't Heavy. It was a man behind Heavy. He moved out of the line of fire. Then Heavy's eyes moved again. He looked at the man on Lawton's left, then at the man on Lawton's right, then back at Lawton.

"You outdraw me and my pals'll fill you so full of lead it'll take a team of mules to drag you out of here."

"You won't see it."

"You Coops are gunfighters. Just goddamn gunfighters."

"Damn right."

Heavy digested that, then, "All right. You can finish your whiskey. Then you're gonna git out of here."

"I don't want your damn whiskey. I'm particular who I drink with."

"All right, you can go. Just git."

"Sure. So you can shoot me in the back."

"Nobody's gonna shoot you in the back."

"Tell your pals to get over here in front of me."

Heavy nodded his head. The men on Lawton's right and left stepped over beside Heavy.

Feeling weak in the knees, but forcing himself to move

73

with dignity, Lawton backed toward the door. It seemed like a mile. He almost couldn't believe it when he was finally outside, out in the fresh air. Still, he didn't dare take his eyes off the open door. Walking backwards wasn't his favorite way of moving, but he had to watch that door. Nobody came out.

He walked backwards to the corner, then turned and ducked around the corner.

Chapter Ten

He didn't sleep much that night. Every sound outside the thin-walled cabin brought him wide awake with a gun in his hand.

He unrolled his bed on the floor opposite the spring bed, with it between him and the door. The door latch wasn't strong enough to stop a big man, but it would at least slow a man down and give Lawton time to grab a gun.

Fully dressed except for his boots, he lay with only the tarp on top of him. The Colt six-gun was under the tarp with him and the Spencer carbine was on the floor within easy reach.

When he thought about it he realized he'd done something dumb. Just plain estupido. What the hell did he accomplish by going back to El Raton? Not one damned thing. Instead he came within a hair of getting himself killed. He lay with his hands under his head and gave himself a silent cussing. What about Mary? You'd throw your life away and leave her a widow with a new child? And Mom? One son has disappeared, accused of every vile crime there is, and then her other son killed in a barroom shootout.

Lawton Coop, you haven't got the brains God gave a jackass. You're lucky you're alive, you dumb yahoo.

By daylight he figured nobody was going to ambush him.

If they'd wanted to sneak up on him they would have done it during the night. He went out to feed his horses, and, still wearing the Colt, walked to the Trinchera Eatery.

Other men stuffing their faces gave him a series of frowns, but said nothing. One man, sitting on his left, got up, paid and went out the door. Another took his place. The man behind the counter brought him his hotcakes, bacon and coffee, and stood there with his hands on his hips.

"From what I hear, we're gonna have to bury you," he said. "You stay around here and your life ain't worth a nickel."

Lawton tried a grin. "I'm beginning to believe it."

"Have you told the sheriff who your next of kin is?"

"Reckon I'd better do that."

The counterman went back to the kitchen.

"Heese offerin' very good advisse, Meester Coop." The voice came from his left. He turned and faced a Mexican wearing cowboy clothes, the same hat, boots and everything a white cowboy would wear. Lawton's eyebrows went up.

"I see whot happen, las night. I wass there."

Lawton saw nothing threatening in the Mexican's face or manner, and turned back to his hotcakes.

"I hear you ast about a poker game that Meester Baylor Coop won."

"Yeah. I was curious about that." His jaw was much better and chewing was easier.

"I wass there. I seen it."

"Yeah?" He stopped chewing. "You did?"

"Si. I wass in town with my compadres on the O.T."

"You ride for the O.T.?"

"Si. Slim and Jake tell about you when they get back two day ago. I knew about you."

His meal was forgotten now. "Tell me about that poker game. What happened."

"Meester Coop won." The Mexican shrugged. "That's all. He play better."

Lawton could speak a little Spanish, but if the Mexican

76

wanted to speak English that was all right with him. "Did he have a lot of luck?"

"Not much for luck. Just play better. A pair of aces, that's all it take to win ever'thing."

"Two aces? Just a pair of bullets?"

"Si. They play stud. One man have two kings showing and another have two jacks. Meester Coop have one ace up." The Mexican smiled, showing strong white teeth. "The man with kings thought Meester Coop bluffing, and the man with jacks try to bluff. Try to make them theenk he have jack in the hole."

"So what happened?"

"I play poker with cowboyss and I know poker. Wot happen is they bluff and raiss and call, and all the money is in the middle of the mesa. The table."

A chuckle came out of Lawton. "And old Bay had 'em wired, huh?"

"Si. Back to back."

Still chuckling, Lawton said, "And he took the jackpot with a pair of bullets. I'll bet that made them madder than a crow on a wet nest."

The Mexican chuckled with him. "They mad, all right. But they have no more money, and Meester Coop go. Leave."

"Ever hear how much he won?"

"A thousand dollar, I theenk."

Lawton chuckled the rest of the way through his breakfast, and when he finished, he said, "If you're still in town tonight, partner, I'd like to buy you a shot of whiskey."

"Got to go. Got a wife and two leetle wans."

"Have you worked for the O.T. long?"

"Since I wass a leetle wan myself."

"Well, thanks a lot, partner."

He was still chuckling when he went out the door and walked to the wagon yard to saddle his dun horse.

Instead of riding down Commerce Street on his way out of

town, he rode across a bridge over the Picketwire and went through the Mexican section. He liked Mexicans. They'd learned how to scratch a living out of this land long before the white men came along. The white settlers could learn a lot from the Mexicans. The Coop family had.

It was another cloudless morning, but Lawton had seen how fast clouds could gather in the high country. One little white cloud would show up on the western horizon. Along would come another. Then the clouds would get together and dump on everything below. And every time the sun went behind a cloud, a cool breeze came up. The temperature could drop ten degrees in a matter of seconds.

Right now the sun was warm on his shoulders and back and getting warmer. The flies were buzzing around his horse's head and biting its neck, and the horse was constantly shaking its head to get them off. Soon, it would be hot. But never as hot as it was in the Pecos Valley.

Pretty country. He could see why Baylor wanted to buy land here. Rough and rocky in places, with arroyos and bluffs, spotted with piñon and cedars. But with good grass, the short kind of grass that would hold its nutrition through the winter.

He had no trouble finding Baylor's cabin, what was left of it. Not a stick was standing. Nothing but a black charred mess of logs. The log foundation told Lawton the cabin had been a small one. Big enough to accommodate a cot and a stove and not much else. A thin steel sheepherder's stove and some pieces of stovepipe were in the middle of the mess. Baylor had built his cabin along a creek that came out of a shallow canyon some six hundred yards west. A pole corral had been torn down and the poles and posts thrown onto the pile of burning logs. East of the cabin a few acres of scrub oak grew along the creek. That would be a good place for cattle to bush up in the winter out of the north wind. In front of the cabin, what Lawton guessed was once the front, the country was fairly level, with at least three different varieties of grass, and wild flowers of every color.

To the north, on the other side of the creek, was a timbered hill, and that was where Baylor had cut the timbers to build his cabin.

Lawton dismounted, squatted on his bootheels and stared at the charred mess. No use digging through it. He tried to picture in his mind Baylor building the place, dragging logs from that hill. Did he have a harness team or did he drag logs with his saddle horses? Building a cabin was a hard job for a man working alone.

The sun was straight overhead now, burning down. The flies were even worse, and Lawton felt sorry for the dun horse. A loose horse would head for some shade where the flies weren't so bad. He'd seen horses stand side by side, head to tail, switching flies off each other's heads. A horse under saddle, especially a sweating horse, caught hell from the flies.

He mounted, brushed a big black fly off the dun's right shoulder, and rode across the creek. Yep, here was where Baylor had dragged logs across. He rode up the creek to the mouth of the canyon, saw nothing interesting there, and turned the dun south. He wasn't looking for anything in particular, just scanning the country out of curiosity. There were rocks of different colors, but nothing that looked like gold. Hell, he wouldn't know gold if he saw it. He was riding across the vega in front of the cabin when he saw the hole in the ground.

Just a small hole. Not as big around as a man's hand. At first glance he thought it was a gopher hole and rode on by. But something about it was different.

Only mildly curious, he reined the horse around and went back. Looked like a hole dug by a pocket gopher. Except for the dim wagon tracks in the grass near the hole. And the black dust around it.

More curious now, Lawton got down to take a closer look. He picked up a pinch of the black dust and studied it. Tasted it. Phoo. Dirt. Black dirt. But fine. Very fine.

Damnedest dirt he ever saw. And the wagon tracks. Did somebody dig this hole? Take an auger of some kind and drill it? Why?

Horseback again, he tried to follow the wagon tracks, but they were too old and too dim. Just a spot here and there where the wheels had sunk into soft dirt. Not being familiar with the soil and vegetation in that part of the country, he couldn't guess how old the tracks were, but they were old. Maybe four months, maybe a year. They seemed to be going south and east, but he couldn't even be sure about that. Looking ahead, he saw a low, rocky ridge that ended a half-mile away. It could be the wagon went around that ridge.

He urged the dun horse into a lope, and when he got to the end of the ridge he studied the ground carefully. No sign of anything on wheels ever having been there. Where did that wagon come from?

Oh well, didn't matter. His stomach was asking for something to digest, and he wished he'd brought along a tortilla or something. The more he thought about it the hungrier he became. Wouldn't a tortilla taste good? It reminded him of the fat Mexican woman who cooked for the Circle C at home. She had a big flat plowshare that she fried tortillas on, and when she spread some refried beans over one of them and rolled it up, it made a right tasty and filling lunch that a cowboy could carry in a saddle pocket.

Nothing better.

He was thinking about that and getting hungrier by the minute when he heard the gunshots.

Chapter Eleven

It was a faint pop-pop away off in the distance. He reined up and listened. There it was again. Pop-pop. Southeast. It sounded like somebody fighting off Indians. Boom. That one was no rifle. More like a shotgun. Boom. The other barrel.

Somebody was shooting at somebody.

It couldn't be Indians. He hadn't heard of any Indian trouble for years. But this was Colorado Territory, and maybe the Indians were still attacking settlers in these parts. If it wasn't Indians, then it was somebody trying to rob somebody. He had to find out.

The dun horse jumped into a run. It pounded over the rocky ground, jumped gulleys, dodged cedars, followed the sound of gunfire. Over a low hill, down and across a deep draw, up another hill, through the trees. Horse and rider crashed through a stand of thick scrub oak, and came out on the edge of a creek. They splashed across the creek and galloped up another hill. There they stopped.

The horse was blowing hard from the run, and the rider was trying to figure out what was happening below. There was a cabin, this one made of rocks like Weepy Willows's cabin. There was a corral and a stock shelter. A cow lay on her side in the corral. The gunfire had stopped.

But only for a moment.

Crack, went a rifle. Boom went a shotgun. He saw them then. There were four men lying on the ground between him and the cabin. On their bellies. A puff of smoke and another crack from a rifle. They were shooting at the cabin. Boom. Somebody in the cabin was shooting back.

Lawton studied the scene carefully. Four men. Nope, there was another back there in the trees, holding their horses. How many in the cabin? More shots. Rifles cracked, the shotgun boomed, and a pop came from the cabin. A pistol. There was a man with a shotgun in the cabin and somebody with a six-gun. Were there a man and woman in there? Or a man and a boy? The men outside were staying out of the range of that scattergun. The pistol wouldn't be much good either at that distance. The attackers had lever-action rifles. They wore wide-brim hats, but they weren't cowboys. Their boots had flat heels, made for walking, not riding.

One of them got to one knee and took careful aim at the cabin. A puff of smoke came out of the rifle barrel. There was no return fire. The slug had to have gone through the window. Lawton hoped nobody was hit.

The man fired again. No dust flew off the cabin rocks. The bullets were going through the window. Still no return fire.

Lawton knew now what was happening. The Maxwell Company had hired gunhands from Denver to drive the settlers off. Those settlers who wouldn't or couldn't pay. These five were hired gunhands. And it was an uneven fight. If they kept it up, they would kill somebody in that cabin.

They hadn't seen Lawton. He reined his horse off the crest of the hill, back the way he'd come. Dismounting, he tried to decide what to do. It was none of his business. The land company had a right to remove trespassers. But he couldn't just stand there with his bare face hanging out and watch hard-working people murdered.

The old Spencer hadn't been fired for months, but he kept the magazine full. He lifted it out of the saddle boot, cocked the hammer back, swung down the finger lever and opened the breech just to be sure. The magazine held seven .56-caliber cartridges. He had no extras. When he slammed the breech closed the action carried a cartridge from the magazine into the firing chamber.

Rifle fire came from below with no answering fire from the cabin. Maybe he was too late.

He went back to the top of the hill, got down on one knee and raised the old Spencer to his shoulder. Paused.

What would Baylor do? Baylor had been in the war. He'd fired a lot of shots at the enemy and he'd no doubt killed men. But not Lawton. Lawton had never fired a gun at anybody. Not even a 'Pache.

The four men below were getting bold now. Two of them stood. They were making targets of themselves to see if anyone was still alive in the cabin and able to shoot. They started walking toward the cabin.

Shoot, damnit, Lawton told himself. He aimed at a spot two yards in front of the man in the lead and squeezed the trigger.

The old Spencer boomed like a cannon and kicked like a mule. But the bullet went where he'd aimed it. The walking men stopped as if they'd run into a wall. They looked back at Lawton, wondering what the hell was going on. Lawton jacked another .56-caliber cartridge into the firing chamber and fired again. He saw dirt fly where the slug hit the ground no more than a yard from a man's boots.

That did it. The two men dropped onto their bellies, and the two already on the ground crawled, clawed and reversed directions. Then they began firing at Lawton. Lead slugs whistled past Lawton's head and screamed off the rocks. Lawton flattened out too, but kept the carbine to his shoulder. He aimed at a rock near one man's head and squeezed off another round. He saw the slug hit the rock and shatter it. The man grabbed his face in both hands and jumped up. The other three watched him and ignored Lawton long enough for the Spencer to boom again. Then they were all running. Running for their horses.

He let them go. He'd fired four rounds and had only three more. His six-gun would be no protection at all against those lever-action rifles. He watched them get to their horses, and realized he was in a lot of danger. In fact, he was in a hell of a spot.

They would circle around behind him and come at him from several directions. He couldn't hold them off. There was only one thing to do, ride like hell for that cabin. But that wasn't very smart either.

He wore a big hat. He was a cowboy. Settlers in that territory hated cowboys.

Maybe his dun horse could outrun them. No, his horse was barefooted and couldn't outrun a shod horse in the rocks. Their horses were no doubt shod. Well, he told himself, do something even if it's wrong, but do something. He got mounted and headed for the cabin.

As the dun horse ran, slid and jumped its way off the hill and into the open space in front of the cabin, Lawton saw a face at the cabin window, saw the twin barrels of the shotgun.

"Friend," he yelled. "I'm a friend." In case they were Mexican he yelled, "Amigo. Amigo, damnit."

He was on the ground before the horse came to a complete stop in front of the window. The bores of the shotgun looked to be as big as the open end of a barn.

Glancing back, he saw he was caught in the middle. Three men with repeating rifles sat their horses on the hill he'd just left, and in front of him was somebody with a double-barreled shotgun. Those rifles couldn't shoot this far, but those yahoos would be coming closer. He had to get inside the cabin, get on the other side of it, or get somewhere.

"I'm a friend," he yelled again.

"Come in. The door's unlocked." The voice was immature. A kid.

He hated to leave his horse standing there, but he figured

84

he had no choice. He tried the door latch. It opened. He stepped inside, carrying the Spencer.

The shotgun was pointed at him and the immature voice demanded, "Who are you? What do you want?"

"I'm . . . I'm not one of them." The light wasn't good in the cabin, and he squinted at the face behind the shotgun. A towheaded kid. Pimply faced. Looking around, Lawton saw a bearded man with his shirt off sitting on the floor against the far wall, holding one hand over his left shoulder. A bloody hand. A woman sat beside him, holding a six-shooter. It was another one-room cabin, bigger than Baylor's had been and with two beds. "I, uh, don't know exactly what's going on here, but I didn't like the looks of things."

"Who are you?" He was about fifteen.

"Listen, son, I'm the gent who chased them off."

"I know that. I saw you, or you wouldn't be in here. Why'd you do that? You're a cowboy."

"Yeah, I'm a cowboy. They're not." He nodded toward the hill. "They're hired gunslingers. And you'd better keep watching out there."

"I know what to do."

"Well, if you're not gonna keep a watch, let me do it. I don't want those gunsels to get too close." With that, Lawton stepped over to the window and looked out. The three horsemen were still on top of the hill. He looked back at the boy. "Is that the best gun you've got?"

"Got a Remington rifle, but it's out of bullets. Ain't been to town for a long time."

"How long have they been shooting at you?"

"Not long. They shot our cow."

Keeping a watch out the window, Lawton asked, "Did they give you any warning?"

The woman spoke for the first time. "Just a piece of paper. And that was two-three months ago. The shurff brung it over." She was middle-aged, thin, tired-looking.

85

"How bad is he hit?"

The man spoke through his beard, "Not bad. Took a ball in the shoulder. Can't move my left arm. But it's a long ways from my heart. I told the boy to holler if they git closer."

Damn, Lawton muttered under his breath. Hell of a note. Got to get those gunsels away from here. He took another look out the window. The three were joined by the fourth, the one who'd been holding the horses. If he took careful aim, he might hit one, and maybe that would send them back to wherever they came from. Their .44-caliber guns, which he guessed they had, wouldn't shoot that far, but the .56 Spencer would. Only three cartridges left. Well, it was worth a try.

He laid the carbine barrel across the windowsill. Held it still and squinted down the barrel. One of the horses was standing broadside, and the man on its back was talking to the others. Lawton got the man's right shoulder in the sights. Steady. Maybe he'd better allow for elevation. He raised the sights to the man's hat, hoping to hit him somewhere between his shoulder and waist. Steady.

The boom of the old Spencer shook the cabin. The horseman on the hill fell off his horse.

"Boy. That's some shootin', Mister." The kid was beside him.

"Yeah. I've got two shots left. Hope those sonsof—bucks don't know that." He jacked another round into the firing chamber.

"They're goin'." The kid was excited now, looking out the window. "They're high-tailin' it. Hey, Pa, they're runnin' off."

They were, in fact. They had the fallen man on his horse, and one man led the horse while another rode alongside and held the injured one in the saddle. Relief swept over Lawton's face. They were leaving. And he hadn't killed anyone. Just wounded one. Maybe not too bad. But now he had this family on his hands.

"Have you got horses?"

"Got two," the boy answered. "Back in a little park behind the house."

"And a wagon?"

"There's a wagon over there by the corral."

"Well, let's hope those gunsels left your horses alone. We've got to get your dad to a doctor. Is there a doctor in Trinidad?"

"I think there is."

The woman moaned, "They shot our cow. She was a good cow. Gave us plenty of milk and butter. They killed her."

"They're mean sonsofbitches," the boy said.

"Well, let's go find your horses."

"We tried to buy the place." The woman was almost in tears. "We couldn't pay much, but we offered to pay some now and the rest later. They said it wasn't for sale."

"They did?" This was puzzling. "They said it wasn't for sale?"

"That's what they said." She went to a big overland trunk at the other end of the room, opened it and took out a sheet of paper. "Steda sellin' it, they had the shurff bring us this."

Lawton took the paper and read it.

NOTICE TO VACATE

To Mr. Ephram Watkins

Your presence is considered to be inimical to the rights of persons and property. You will be given until July 1 to arrange your business affairs and go. You must not be found here after that day. This means business. Take warning.

Horace Willard
Sheriff, Las Animas County
Territory of Colorado

"Well, I'll be d—danged," Lawton muttered. "Wonder if Baylor got a notice like this."

"Who?"

"Baylor Coop."

"You know Baylor Coop?" The boy was excited again.

"Yeah. Do you know him?"

"Sure. He was our neighbor."

"He was a good neighbor," the woman said. "He brought us fresh venison and we gave him some fresh butter. Yes, he did get a notice like that."

"Well, I'll be danged."

"Where'd you know Baylor Coop?" the boy asked.

"At home. Southern New Mexico. He's my brother."

"Gosh-dang." The boy was so excited he almost couldn't stand it. "Did you hear that, Pa? This here's Baylor Coop's brother."

The man's eyes were squinched closed and his face was screwed up in pain, but he managed to mutter, "He's a good man, Baylor Coop, wherever he is."

"He took Thomas huntin' with 'im," the woman said, "and showed 'im how to shoot this old six-shooter."

"He was the best with a gun I ever did see. No wonder you could knock a man off his horse away out there. You're Baylor Coop's brother."

"Yeah." Lawton had other things on his mind. "Did you say they wouldn't sell this land to you?" He squinted at the woman as if he couldn't believe her.

"No. They said it wasn't for sale."

He digested that, then, "Well, we've got to get your dad to town. Let's go find those horses."

But before he went out the door, he asked again, "You offered them cash money?"

"What money we've got."

"Damn," he muttered as he stepped outside. "There's something strange about this whole deal.

"Damned strange."

Chapter Twelve

They found the horses on the other side of a small creek. To get there they walked through three acres of green crops, planted in rows. An irrigation ditch had been cut with a walking plow from the creek to the crops, carrying water. Only the tops of the crops showed above the ground, and Lawton didn't recognize them.

They took the mattress and some blankets from one of the beds and laid them in the back of a light wagon. They got the man to lie on them. The woman sat beside him, and the boy drove the team. Lawton rode along on the dun.

It was ten or twelve miles to town, but the boy followed a wagon road that went around the rough places, and by late afternoon they were on the outskirts of Trinidad. On the way, Lawton rode alongside the wagon, asking questions.

"Where did you folks come from?"

"Kansas. They said land was free out here and we came to stake our claim."

"You say you got that notice last spring?"

The boy answered, "It was around the first of April, I think. The sheriff brought it out."

"Do you know when Baylor got his notice?"

"He got his sooner. A long time ago. I don't recollect exactly when."

"Hmm. Have you seen any holes drilled in the ground? Little holes."

"Yeah, there's two of 'em on our place, and I seen some more up north."

"Do those holes have black dirt around them?"

"The ones on our place have."

"Do you know what they are, what they were drilled for?"

"I ain't never seen anything like 'em before. Have you, Ma?"

"No, I ain't, and neither has Ephram."

"Do you know what they are, Mister Coop?"

Lawton shook his head. "No. I've never seen anything like them either. Did you see who drilled them?"

"Naw. We didn't know they was there until early this spring."

"Hmm."

The doctor was easy to find. He had a three-room adobe house with a sign on a post outside. The sign said: "Doctor Hiram Bromley. M.D. Ph.D. D.D.S."

"With all those credentials," Lawton mused, "he surely knows what he's doing."

He was a young man with a thin moustache, a potbelly and red suspenders to hold his pants up. Thick curly hair grew low on his forehead. "Bring him in here. Lay him on this cot."

They got Ephram Watkins on the cot, and while the doctor looked him over, Lawton looked around the room. There was a shelf containing a half-dozen medical books, but there was no framed diploma.

"Bullet wound, eh?" Doctor Bromley probed Ephram's shoulder with his fingers. The patient's face screwed up in pain. "Let's see now, a shot of morphia ought to make you feel better." He opened a dresser drawer and took out a syringe, then took a syringe needle from a jar of alcohol. He filled the syringe from another jar, rubbed some alcohol on the patient's right arm, and stuck the needle in. "Hurts for a second but pretty soon you won't feel anything."

The patient winced, and so did Lawton. "Gosh," the boy said. "Poor Ephram," the woman said.

"Let's see now, need some scissors, an artery forceps and a scalpel. Have to open it up and see how much damage is done. Have to get the bullet out." He looked over his shoulder at the woman and boy. "Perhaps you should wait outside."

They left. Lawton started to leave with them.

"You, sir, would you mind staying? I might need you to hold him down."

"All right, but I thought that morphia was supposed to stop the pain."

"Oh, it will. If it doesn't, I've got some chloroform. But we'll see." He bent over the patient with a scalpel in his hand. A quick slice, and the shoulder was open to the bone. The patient tried to jump up, but Lawton held him down.

"It hurt him, doctor. Can't you keep from hurting him?"

"It takes a while for the morphia to take effect."

Silently, Lawton wondered why the doctor didn't wait, but he said no more.

"Uh-huh. The bullet hit the bone and broke off a shard. Hand me those forceps, will you please."

Lawton handed him the long-handled forceps and watched while the doctor picked a hunk of lead and pieces of bone out of the patient's flesh. The patient was quiet now.

"I think I got it all. Now I have to tie off the bleeding." The doctor worked with swift fingers. "There. Now I'll sew him up, and he'll live. He'll have a very sore shoulder for a time, and his shoulder will never be as strong as it once was, but it won't be useless either."

"Sir," Lawton said, "have you doctored any other bullet wounds today?"

"Not today. Why?"

91

"This man was shot by some hoodlums, and I shot one of them."

"Then it must have been a fatal wound."

"But I saw him on a horse after I shot him."

"Sometimes it takes a while for the vital organs to stop working."

He was relieved to be outside. The woman and boy stood beside their wagon. "How is he?" The woman's voice quavered. "Is he all right?"

"The doctor said he'll have a sore shoulder, but he'll live. What are you folks gonna do? Can I help you any?"

"Reckon we'll go back if Ephram can move."

"Better wait 'till tomorrow. He's still under the morphia."

"We can camp around here somewhere, Ma."

Lawton said, "Go over to the wagon camp. I'm going over there now and I'll fix it up with the owner so you can put your team in a stable and sleep in a cabin. Have you got grocery money?"

"Yeah, we've got a little money saved up. We were gonna buy some land with it, but now . . ." The woman shrugged.

"I'll fix it up for you at the wagon camp." Lawton mounted the dun and rode away.

He made arrangements for the Watkins family and their horses, paid for them for the night, then went looking for the sheriff. Not in. Wouldn't you know it. Well, hell. What now?

He'd have given good money to know why the Maxwell Land Company refused to sell a few acres to the Watkinses. They were supposed to be in the business of selling land. And those holes in the ground. They meant something. What?

Hell, go see Benjamin Mock and ask him. He seems to be a decent sort. He walked to the bank. Closed. Aw, hell.

Stomping back to the wagon yard, he passed the Las Animas Gazette, saw the publisher and his daughter working inside, turned and went in. He told them about the attack on the Watkins's cabin and the wounding of Ephram Watkins. "I don't know whether that's news," he said, "but in case it is, Mrs. Watkins and her son are staying at the wagon camp tonight."

James C. Gordon shook his head. "It's happened several times in the past year. But I suppose we ought to have something in the paper about it."

Annie Gordon picked up a sheaf of paper and two lead pencils from the desk. "I'll go over to the wagon yard and interview Mrs. Watkins."

"Does the sheriff ever do anything about this?" Lawton asked.

"No. He says those people have no right to be there, and they were given fair warning."

Lawton was happy to be talking to knowledgeable people, to have someone to talk to, and he talked on. He told the Gordons what Mrs. Watkins had said about trying to buy the land and being refused, and he told them about the holes in the ground.

James C. Gordon looked over his glasses at Lawton. "The reason they give is they're running cattle over there and they plan to bring a herd of cattle up from Texas and they need a lot of grazing land. They'll sell most of the Maxwell grant, but not all of it."

Annie Gordon had started to leave, but now she waited and listened.

"Uh-huh. Have you heard anything about those holes in the ground?"

"No. That's something I haven't heard of, and I thought I'd heard of just about everything around here."

"This is very mysterious," the girl said.

"Sure is. Uh, Miss Gordon, did you . . . in your conversations with Baylor, did he say anything about trying to buy the land and being refused?"

93

"He said he did buy it. And I believe him."

"The more I think about it, the more I'm convinced he bought it. Not that I ever had any doubts. If he said he bought it, he bought it. What happened is, he won a pile of money in a poker game and paid for some land. When the gents he won the money from wanted a chance to win it back, he had to tell them he'd spent it. What he spent it on was land. He'd built a cabin and one thing and another and was planning to prove up on it, and when he found out it belonged to the Maxwell Land Company, he paid for it."

Annie Gordon was nodding her head. "Uh-huh, uh-huh. That's logical. I'd bet anything that's exactly what happened. But"—her forehead furrowed—"why wasn't there a record of it in the county clerk's office?"

Lawton put into words something that had been on his mind. "Somebody took it."

"Uh-huh. But who? And why?"

"The county clerk sure didn't gain anything by it. He's dead. What was his name?"

"Orville Jackson. I think he was honest. Too bad he had tuberculosis."

"What do you think, Mr. Gordon, was Orville Jackson honest?"

"I'm sure of it. He was dying and he knew it."

"Did he, uh, he didn't live alone, did he?"

"No," Annie Gordon answered, "he had a housekeeper. A Mrs. Willis."

"Is she still in town?"

"Yes. I saw her in the mercantile a few days ago. If you want to see her, I can show you where she lives. She probably won't be at home right now, though. She's working for Benjamin Mock now. You'll have to wait until tomorrow morning."

"Well." Lawton rubbed his jaw, realized he needed a shave, studied the floor. "I don't know what I'd gain by it, but, sure, why not. Yeah, I might as well go see her."

"I'll go with you."

"Well, there are some people around town who don't like me very much. Going with me could be dangerous."

"I'm not afraid."

"Annie," Mr. Gordon said, "perhaps you shouldn't be so . . ."

"If Mr. Coop—Lawton—will let me, I'm going."

Chapter Thirteen

He wrote a letter to Mary, telling her he hoped to start for home in a few days. He said he had reason to believe that Baylor was alive and well, but he had no clue as to his whereabouts. He didn't mention the crimes Baylor was accused of. Trying to make his letter cheerful and worry-free he told about the climate in southern Colorado Territory and the terrain. A good place to raise cattle, and a good place to live, he said. Of course, he admitted, he didn't know what it was like in the winter.

At the camp owner's cabin, he was told the postoffice was a small room in the mercantile, and the postmistress was a Mrs. Miller whose husband owned the mercantile. She sorted the mail and handed it to the addressees when they asked for it.

Just like home. At White Lake, named after a wide spot in the Little Hondo River, old Mrs. Ables sorted the mail and knew all the news before the addressees did. No one doubted she held the envelopes up to a light so she could see what was inside, and no one doubted she had even opened the mail at times. But no one complained because Mrs. Ables was a good old soul. When the letter came telling about John Prichard being killed in the war, Mrs. Ables delivered it to the widow herself and sat up all night with her and prayed with her. And when the war was over and Baylor wrote that he was coming home, she sent her nephew on horseback to the Circle C Ranch to deliver the good news. The boy, only twelve or thirteen, was so excited he told Mrs. Coop all about it before he remembered to give her the letter.

Thinking about Mrs. Ables and White Lake brought a chuckle out of Lawton as he walked back to his cabin. But then, come to think of it, that explained something.

That explained why Baylor hadn't written home for so long. He was a wanted man. Wanted badly. It wouldn't do to have some busybody postmaster or postmistress read the letter. It would be the same as telling every lawman in Colorado Territory and all points west where he was. The only reason the lawmen hadn't been to the Circle C to look for him was they had no idea he was from there. But if Mrs. Ables saw a letter from him the word would spread until a lawman heard about it.

Baylor would do anything to keep the sheriff and the U.S. marshals from bothering his mother.

And now that Lawton was thinking about it, would Mrs. Ables read his letter to Mary? If she did, everyone in White Lake would soon know he was in Colorado looking for Baylor. Would that make some lawman curious? Well, he would have to chance it. He couldn't let Mary worry.

He walked to the mercantile and found it closed. From there he went to the café and had boiled potatoes and beef. The counterman didn't say anything about the shooting at the Watkins's homestead, and he guessed that that piece of news hadn't been spread yet. The newspaperman and his daughter wouldn't mention it. They'd rather have folks read about it in their newspaper.

Back at the wagon camp, he hunted up the Watkinses to see how they were doing. He found the doctor just leaving their rented cabin. "He was in so much pain that I gave him another injection of morphia," the doctor said. "But I warned them that I can't give him another. It's habit-forming. It can get to be a terrible habit."

"Maybe he'll feel better after a good night's sleep," Lawton said.

"Possibly. But he will be in some pain for a few days."

Lawton muttered, "Those sonsofbitches."

"Beg your pardon."

"Oh, I was cussing the hired gunslingers who did this to him."

"Have you reported this to the sheriff?"

"No. But I will as soon as I can find him."

"Good evening, sir."

Again, he slept on the floor with the bed between him and the door. He kept the Colt six-gun handy. At daylight, he fed his horses and made another trip to the café. Still, there was nothing said about a shooting at the Watkins homestead. From there he went to the mercantile and posted his letter to Mary. It would go out early next morning on the southbound stage, he was told. The southbound from Pueblo got into Trinidad in the early night, but the Raton Pass was so narrow and dangerous they waited until daylight to go on south. Out of curiosity, he asked how long it took the northbound stage to get to Pueblo. Most of the day, he was told. It left about the middle of the morning and got to Pueblo soon after dark. About twelve hours. A trip to Denver took three days on the stage, and anyone going on horseback could expect to take four or five days. The stageline had relay stations with fresh teams waiting.

The postmistress was talkative. "In a few years, we'll be able to go to Denver in one day. When the railroad gets here. Won't that be grand?"

"I hear a railroad is coming," Lawton allowed, "but I haven't heard when."

"We don't know for sure, but we know it's coming. There's

so much talk about it, it has to be true. In fact, there's talk that two railroads are coming, one from the north and one from the east. They'll both get to Trinidad unless one goes broke."

"Takes a lot of money to build a railroad."

"It surely does. A powerful lot of money. Say, you're not . . . are you?"

"Good day, madam."

The sheriff wasn't in and the door was locked. "Hell with him," Lawton muttered as he walked away. What now? Oh yeah, go see that Mrs. Willis, the dead county clerk's housekeeper. Don't know what good it'll do but have to do something. Annie Gordon said she wants to go along. She knows Mrs. Willis. Maybe she can help.

The girl was alone in the Gazette's brick building, looking as pretty as ever. "It's only a short walk. I'll take some notepaper just in case."

"I doubt there'll be any news in this visit," Lawton said, "but what do I know about news?"

"You made some news yesterday. I went over to interview Mrs. Watkins early this morning, and she told me all about the attack on their house. It will be in tomorrow's paper. We started setting type last night."

Mrs. Willis lived in a two-room board-and-batten house two blocks from Commerce Street. A narrow outhouse was in back, between the house and a shallow arroyo. A split-rail fence surrounded the front yard, and flowers grew inside the fence. There were two rosebushes, yellow flowers, blue flowers and big round lavender ones. Mariposas, the girl said. They grew wild in the mountains, and Mrs. Willis had transplanted some in her yard. Other women had tried that and failed, but Mrs. Willis had a gift for growing things.

She answered within a few seconds of Annie Gordon's knock. A pleasantly plump woman of about fifty, with gray hair. She smiled a pleasant smile.

99

"Good morning, Mrs. Willis," the girl said. "I have a friend with me who would like to talk to you, if you don't mind."

"Good morning, Annie. Come in." She stepped back to allow Annie and Lawton to enter. Lawton habitually took off his hat and wiped his boots on the doormat before entering. The room was comfortable with two stuffed chairs and a stuffed sofa. A rock fireplace was built into one corner. Though the floor was bare wood, it was spotless.

"Won't you sit down?" They both sat on the sofa, Annie with her hands folded on her lap and Lawton with his hat on his lap.

"How are you, Mrs. Willis?" the girl asked. "Are you feeling all right? I heard you had a summer cold."

"Oh, I'm fine now. I had a little head cold for a time, but it's gone."

"Mrs. Willis, I would like to introduce you to Mr. Lawton Coop. He is the brother of Baylor Coop."

Immediately, the atmosphere turned cold. Lawton stood to be introduced and opened his mouth to speak, but when he saw the pinched bitter expression that came over Mrs. Willis's face, he just stood there with his mouth open.

"Did you say Baylor Coop?" The older woman's voice shook. "That terrible man. That terrible, terrible man."

The girl started to say something, but kept quiet. Lawton didn't know what to say.

The older woman gasped, "He . . . he robbed me. He robbed everybody. He took every dollar I had."

"Mrs. Willis . . ."

The girl was cut off. "When he robbed the bank he took every dollar I had and left me with nothing."

"Uh, Mrs. Willis," Lawton put in weakly, "I'm not so sure Baylor robbed the bank. He wouldn't steal from anybody and he sure wouldn't steal from a woman."

"I saw him." Mrs. Willis jumped up and stamped her foot. Her face was red.

"You saw him?"

"Of course. I was just cleaning up for Mr. Mock when he came to the door. I heard him tell Mr. Mock to go to the bank with him or he would kill him. I . . ." Anger was making her short of breath and she had to stop talking for a moment. Then, "I . . . when they left I went to get Sheriff Spates. I hurried as fast as I could, but Mr. Spates lived away over on the east side of town, and . . ."

"I know you were there," the girl said. "You told me about it the next day. But are you sure?"

"Ever since Mr. Jackson died I've been going over to Mr. Mock's house in the afternoons to clean and cook supper. He had visitors that night and a late supper. I was just about to leave when that . . . that terrible man came."

"Are you sure it was Baylor?" Lawton asked.

"Of course. I'd seen him before. I'd seen him in the mercantile and in the bank and in Mr. Jackson's house."

"What was he doing in Mr. Jackson's house?"

She snapped. "I don't know. I didn't listen. It was none of my business."

"When was that?"

"The day before poor Mr. Jackson passed away."

Lawton could think of nothing to say to that. The girl was quiet too.

"You're . . . you're his brother?"

"Yes, Mrs. Willis, I am, and I still don't think . . ."

"Then, sir, I must ask you to leave my home."

Lawton shuffled his feet. "Sure, Mrs. Willis. I'm sorry I, we, bothered you."

He couldn't get to the door fast enough. The girl was right behind him.

Outside on the street, he could only shake his head sadly and look at the ground.

"She's a widow," the girl said. "Her husband was working on the toll road over Raton Pass when he was killed. He left her this house and a little money. Now the money is gone."

101

"I'm sorry for her," Lawton said, still looking down. "I can't blame her for being mad at Baylor."

"I'm sorry for her too," the girl said. "She has had some rotten luck."

He shook his head again. "I'm trying to find evidence to clear my brother's name and all I've done is find more evidence against him."

Chapter Fourteen

This required a lot of thinking. The whole thing didn't make sense. Sometime, somewhere, something had happened that he hadn't heard about, and whatever it was, it was the key to the whole damned puzzle. He would have to go over it all in his mind. Start at the beginning and study every piece of information he had picked up.

He walked with Annie Gordon to the newspaper building and went back to the wagon camp, planning to ride the pack horse up into the hills somewhere. He did his best thinking on horseback.

While he was saddling his horse he saw young Thomas Watkins feeding the family's team of horses. "How's your dad?"

"He hurts, but he's better than he was last night before I went for the doctor."

"What are you going to do?"

"We're goin' back as soon as Pa is better. We've got crops to harvest."

"I saw something growing there, but I couldn't tell what it was."

"Spuds and turnips and carrots and cabbages."

"Does that stuff grow around there?"

"Had a fair to middlin' crop last year and this year looks better."

Lawton tightened the cinch on the bay pack horse, and though the horse was plumb gentle, he habitually turned it around once to let it get the feel of the saddle before he put his foot in the stirrup. "If I can help you, let me know."

He rode down Commerce Street this time, heading west. Let the whole damned town see him. If anybody wants another fight with the Coop family, let them step up and say so. The Coop family didn't have a damned thing to be ashamed of, no matter what that widow woman saw. The more he thought about it, the madder he got. To hell with the whole damned town and everybody in it. Except maybe the Gordons. They seemed like honest, decent folks. But everybody else could go to hell.

Riding past the Merchants Bank, he remembered that he wanted to ask Benjamin Mock why the land company refused to sell the Watkinses their homestead. He remembered too the explanation given by the newspaperman, James C. Gordon. All right, that wasn't hard to believe. But he also wanted to ask Benjamin Mock about those holes in the ground. He turned the horse around, went back, dismounted and tied the horse to a hitchrail.

Mr. Mock wasn't in, the young receptionist said. He went to Pueblo on business and wouldn't be back until the next day.

"Are there any other officers of the land company in town?" he asked. "I'd like some information about land sales."

"No, the others live elsewhere. Some in Denver and some in the east."

"How about the ranch? Who owns that?"

"Oh, Mr. Springs owns the ranch, but he doesn't live there. He has a ranch manager named Rowe, Ward Rowe, but Mr. Rowe has nothing to do with land sales. Mr. Springs lives in Denver."

Lawton stood before her desk with his hat in his hands. "Is Benjamin Mock the only one who can sell land on the Maxwell grant?"

"Yes sir. He is in charge of that."

"Well, thanks just the same."

Horseback again, he followed the Picketwire River, going nowhere in particular. He'd heard about that river. Its real name was the Purgatoree, or Purgatwah, or something like that. Most folks called it the Picketwire because that was easier to say. He rode along the top of a deep arroyo cut through the land by the river, stopped and looked down at the water a moment and then across the arroyo. The far bank was steep and a strange color. Good brown soil on top, but under that the soil was black. Strange-looking.

A mile farther he passed a small farm with rows of crops of some kind sprouting a few inches above the ground. A Mexican in a big straw sombrero worked with a hoe among the rows. Like the Watkins's crops, this too was irrigated with water from the river. The Mexicans knew how to irrigate. They'd been doing that for many years.

He turned his horse in that direction, wanting to be friendly, but when the Mexican looked up and saw him, he dropped the hoe and hurried to his rock cabin. Aw hell, Lawton said under his breath. Turning the horse around, he rode away at a trot.

Riding aimlessly, now at a walk, he found himself going south into the rough country, heading toward the remains of Baylor's cabin. He went over in his mind everything he had learned since coming to Colorado. Questions came to his mind. Questions, questions, questions. Like, why did Baylor allow himself to be arrested and thrown in jail? Baylor bought his land fair and square, and he wouldn't allow any lawman to arrest him for refusing to leave it. Not without somebody getting killed. The Coop brothers had been brought up to respect law and order, but they had been made to realize that the law wasn't always fair, and some of the lawmen were just as crooked as the criminals. How about Sheriff William Spates? What kind of a man was he?

Without intending to, he found himself at the bottom of the canyon that led to Weepy Willows's claim. He stopped, thinking. He'd like to talk to the old man again. Why? Well, maybe he knew something he didn't mention before. Aw, not likely. Well, maybe. He had to do something. Might as well try. He wondered if the old sourdough would fire another warning shot at him, or if he'd recognize him. Bullets flying anywhere near wasn't his idea of fun, but . . .

He rode up the canyon, following a game trail that had seen little traffic. At the top, he stopped and looked around. He saw the pile of boulders that Willows had been hiding behind a couple of days earlier, but there was no sign of the old man now. Lawton waited, yelled, "Hello. Hello, Mr. Willows." No answer.

Riding at a slow walk, he went around the boulders to where he could see the cabin. Stopped again. "Hello. It's Lawton Coop." Went, slowly, cautiously, stopped in front of the cabin. "Hello."

It would be bad manners to dismount without being invited in, but maybe the old man was sick, or hurt. He was trying to decide what to do when he heard a voice behind him.

"Hyo-o, young feller."

Startled, he twisted in his saddle and looked back. Weepy Willows was right behind him, carrying the Henry rifle over his shoulder, grinning through his gray beard.

"I was beginning to think you weren't at home."

"Saw you comin' from up there, but I recognized you. Git down and come in."

Lawton dismounted and tied the bay to the same tree he'd tied his dun horse to. He followed the old man inside.

"I was just fixin' to fry up some spuds and onions and a piece of sirloin. Set, and purty soon we'll eat." Willows opened a small burlap bag, took out a couple of potatoes.

106

"I can't cook as well as you do," Lawton said, "but I can at least peel the spuds." He opened his pocketknife and picked up a potato. "I'm still trying to figure out what happened to my brother. Excuse me for asking so many questions, but how many times did you see him?"

"Oh, two, maybe three times." Willows busied himself unwrapping a hind quarter of venison from a sheet of canvas. He sniffed of the meat, then took a long butcher knife from the table and began slicing off two flat pieces.

"When was the last time?"

"Right after he broke out of jail."

"Oh? He told you about busting out of jail then?"

"Yeah. Said they tricked 'im. He stayed overnight here to let his horse rest, then borrowed some grub and lit out early in the mornin'. I tole 'im he could stay a while, but he said he didn't want to cause me any trouble."

Lawton finished peeling two potatoes and reached for another one that was on the windowsill over the stove.

"Don't peel that one."

"Why?" He noticed then that the vegetable had already been split lengthwise.

"That's my quicksilver spud."

"Huh? What's that?"

The old man took a bandana out of a hip pocket and wiped his wet eyes. "It's what I used to separate the color from the quicksilver. It's . . . well, first I went to the crik and panned out as much of the worthless dirt as I could, then put in a little quicksilver and let the color stick to it, then I put it in that there spud. I hollowed out the spud and put the stuff in, then wired it shut and cooked the hell out of 'er."

"Gold sticks to quicksilver, is that it?"

"Yup. Lookee here." He reached into his pants pocket and produced a yellow rock about half as big as his thumb. "This's what I got out of 'er."

Lawton took the nugget and looked closely at it. "I'll be damned."

107

"See, the quicksilver melts a lot faster than gold does, and soaks into the spud. That's why you don't wanta eat that spud. It'd kill you."

"Yeah?"

"I squeezed as much as I could out of it 'cuz the stuff costs good money, but I make sure I don't get any of it on what I eat."

"It's poison, huh?"

"That's what they say. I never seen anybody die from it, but I heered about it. I heered about a feller that got some down, and his guts turned inside out and he choked to death on his own blood."

"That would make a man mighty careful, all right. Are two spuds enough? Shall I slice them and put them in this skillet?"

"Unless you wanta eat like a hound dog. Here, I'll put some onions in the skillet with 'em."

Lawton stepped back and let the old man finish the cooking. "You say my brother was tricked somehow?"

"That's what he said. Said the sheriff came to his claim and told 'im if he'd go to town with 'im, they'd get it all straight about who owns what land and ever'thing would be hunky-dorey, so he went with 'im."

"Uh-huh. So that's how they got him to leave peacefully."

"Yup. But he didn't trust 'im, see. Said he made 'im stay in front of 'im all the way to town, but when they got there, he found hisself with five or six guns pointed at 'im."

Lawton dropped into a chair and slapped the table. "That explains something that has been puzzling me. I knew he wouldn't leave his land peacefully unless there was some trickery."

"That's what they done. They tricked 'im. But he busted out and got his horse and high-tailed it up here. I never trusted the John Laws myself, and I staked 'im to some grub." Willows had the potatoes and onions frying in bacon fat now, and he stirred them with a large spoon. The odor of frying onions reminded Lawton that it had been too long since breakfast.

"Did he say where he was going from here?"

"Said he didn't know hisself."

"That was the last time you saw him?"

Wiping his eyes with the bandana again, the old man gave Lawton a sad liquid stare. "Yup. I always wondered what happened to 'im, and then last winter I went down to town and heered about the bank bein' robbed and the sheriff gittin' killed. I don't know if that boy done it, but if he did I'll bet he had a good reason."

"Yeah. If the sheriff tricked him once he probably did it again. Or tried to. If Baylor killed the sheriff it was self-defense."

Taking two tin plates out of a box nailed to the wall, Weepy Willows set the table, then spooned the frying potatoes and onions to one side in the big iron skillet and dropped in the meat. "It don't make no matter. A man that kills a lawdog is gonna be hung as quick as he's caught." He sprinkled some salt on the meat.

"Yeah." Lawton brushed some flies away from his plate. "That's the way it is, all right."

The meal was a little too greasy, but it was filling. When the plates were empty, Lawton carried a bucket of water from the creek and despite the old man's protest, insisted on washing the dishes. Then he went to his horse and untied the reins.

"It's none a my business, young feller, but what're you gonna do now?"

"Go back to town. Listen, can I bring you some chuck or anything? I've got two horses and a pack outfit, and I can bring you anything you need. In case you don't want to go to town yourself."

"Naw. Thanks just the same. I haveta go down once in a while just so I don't forget what civilization looks like. How long're you gonna stay?"

"As long as it takes. You answered one of my questions today. I'll keep looking around and asking, and maybe I'll find some more answers."

"Mebbe you'll still be there the next time I go down. If you are you can help me spend some a these little rocks."

Grinning, Lawton said, "I'll probably be there, asking questions."

He mounted. "Yep, I've got a hell of a lot of questions to ask."

Chapter Fifteen

It was dark by the time he got back to Trinidad, but when he rode past the Las Animas Gazette he saw the publisher and his daughter working inside. He reined up and went in. They were so busy rolling the press over the flat bed of type that they didn't see him. James C. Gordon was pulling a long handle that rolled the press, and Annie Gordon was cutting off the printed sheets and folding them. Lawton wished he hadn't come in. They didn't have time to talk to him and he didn't really have anything to talk about anyway. He wondered if he could leave without being seen.

"Oh." The girl jumped as if she'd been goosed in the rear when she spotted him. "Lawton. You startled me."

Her father looked up, nodded a greeting and kept on working.

"I didn't mean to. I'm sorry I bothered you. I didn't know you were so busy."

"Got to get the paper out." Her fingers were black with ink. "Look at this." She held up a freshly printed sheet. A big black headline yelled:

HOMESTEADER ATTACKED AND WOUNDED

Below that:

Mr. Ephram Watkins, his wife and son, were attacked by riflemen Wednesday at their homestead on Kettle Creek. Mr. Watkins suffered a gunshot wound in the left shoulder before the attackers retreated.

They were aided in their defense by Mr. Lawton Coop of southern New Mexico Territory who happened to be in the area and heard gunshots. It is believed a shot from Mr. Coop's heavy caliber rifle wounded or killed one of the attackers. Doctor Hiram Bromley said he treated Mr. Watkins's wound, but no other gunshot victims have been reported to him. This leads Sheriff Horace Willard to believe the injured attacker died of his wound.

Mrs. Watkins related that they were attacked without warning, and the armed ruffians shot and killed their milk cow. They took refuge in their cabin, but soon ran out of rifle ammunition and were trying to hold off the attackers with a shotgun and revolver when Mr. Coop came along and helped drive them off.

Mrs. Watkins stated that they were warned by Sheriff Willard last fall that they were trespassing on land belonging to the Maxwell Land Company and would have to leave. She related that they tried to buy the land, but Mr. Benjamin Mock, who is in charge of land sales for the company, refused to sell it to them. Mr. Mock was out of town Thursday and could not be reached for comment.

The Watkins family settled on the land two years ago last spring, believing it to be public domain. When they were told the land is part of the Maxwell grant, they didn't believe it at first. But Mrs. Watkins said that when they were finally convinced that they were on privately owned land they tried to do the right thing and buy fifty acres.

The incident is not the first of its kind. Last fall, Mr. George Winton and his wife and infant were attacked in a similar manner at their homestead two miles farther west on Kettle Creek. Mr. Winton was killed, and their cabin was later burned to the ground. Their attackers were never identified.

Sheriff Willard said he does not condone such attacks, and if the hoodlums are identified he will arrest them. However, he said the land does legally belong to the Maxwell Land Company, and . . .

Lawton lowered the paper and looked at the girl. "This is telling what happened, all right. That's what a newspaper is supposed to do."

"Well, we, my father and I, decided not to mention that you are the brother of Baylor Coop, but some people will realize that, and we could be putting you in more danger. I hope not."

"So be it."

"We believe in naming names, as you can see. Mr. Mock, when he reads this, will be outraged. He can cause us some problems with the merchants, and without their advertising we wouldn't be able to earn a living."

"I don't know anything about journalism, but it seems to me you wouldn't be doing your job if you didn't name names."

"That's the way we feel about it."

"Well"—he folded the paper and handed it back to her—"don't worry about me. If anything happens I won't blame you." Now his fingers were black with ink too.

"I'm relieved that you feel that way, Mr., uh, Lawton. But be careful, will you?"

He wrote another letter to Mary. He could see her in his mind, and he would have given anything to touch her. He felt a powerful need to communicate with her. The lamplight in his rented cabin was so dim he had to sit close to it and hold

113

the tablet of paper on his lap. How he wished he could talk to her. He wanted to tell her everything. She would understand. She knew Baylor, knew he was honest and honorable. She would see that her husband's heart was heavy, and her wide gray eyes would be full of sympathy. She would hug him and tell him how much she loved him.

Stopping twice to sharpen the lead pencil with his pocketknife, he wrote it all down. Everything. At the end he had to admit, as much as he hated to, that Baylor did rob the bank. "Please don't tell mother," he wrote. "There is more to this than I know. I wish I could start home tomorrow, but I must stay and find out exactly what happened. I believe that when the whole truth is known, Baylor won't look so bad." He told her too about killing a man. He had never even pointed a gun at anyone before, and now he had killed a man. Someone he didn't know. He didn't even know his name. Mary, like him, had come from a pioneering family, and would understand. She would try to make him feel better.

He wrote on, and when he was finished he read it over carefully. Then he tore it up.

It wouldn't do. Mrs. Ables might read it and then his mother would know. His mother would worry herself sick. He had to keep it to himself.

The *Las Animas Gazette* caused a stir in the town, but not much. At breakfast, the counterman wanted to know what kind of rifle Lawton had, and Lawton told him.

"I've seen them guns. A Yankee gun. I'm from Missoura, and I never seen one of them Spencers till after the war."

"There are new rifles now that will shoot a lot faster. Winchester repeating rifles, they're called. I think that's what those gunslammers had. But they shoot .44s, and I don't think they'll carry much farther than a .44 pistol cartridge."

Other customers listened to the conversation and looked

Lawton over, but said nothing.

"That young doc, whatsisname, took the lead out of Watkins and sewed 'im up, huh?"

"Yeah. Gave him a couple shots of morphia to keep him quiet. Where did he come from anyway?"

"Dunno. Chicago, I think."

The counterman had work to do and left Lawton to finish his hotcakes and sausage in peace.

The sheriff's office was unlocked. Surprise. Before he went in, Lawton decided he wasn't going to allow himself to be bawled out for not reporting the gun battle. Surprise again. Sheriff Horace Willard said nothing about it. He was sitting at his desk with his boots resting on an open desk drawer, his wide-brim hat tilted back on his head.

"Mornin', son. Purty day."

"Yeah," Lawton said, trying to be amiable, "but I saw one little cloud over west, and judging from what I've learned about this climate, it could swell up and get somebody wet." He sat in the other chair and crossed his legs.

"It could, but nobody'd complain. Rain makes things grow. What're you up to this mornin'?"

"Same thing. Asking questions."

"You been askin' a lot of questions. Who're you gonna harangue today?"

"I'll start with you. You weren't sheriff when Baylor was arrested and busted out of jail and all that, but you lived around here and you heard all about it."

Sheriff Horace Willard raised his hat and scratched his balding head. "Yeah?"

"He did bust out, didn't he? And when did County Clerk Orville Jackson die? Did he die before or after Baylor busted out?"

"What's that got to do with anything?"

"Maybe nothing. I'm just grabbing at flies, hoping to catch something."

"Why do you wanta know?"

115

"Because Baylor was tricked into coming to town and getting arrested, and I'll bet there was trickery in the whole damned shooteree."

"What makes you think that?"

Lawton was becoming exasperated. The sheriff was asking questions, not answering them. "I know Baylor."

"And what makes you think he was tricked into gettin' arrested?"

He stood. "Aw, forget it." He was out the door before the sheriff could say anything more.

Annie Gordon was carrying an armload of newspapers and selling them on the street. She was selling them fast, filling a pocket of her long dress with copper pennies. Pedestrians were standing on the sidewalk reading the paper as horsedrawn wagons and buggies creaked and groaned past on the hard-packed dirt street.

"Morning, Annie."

"Good morning, Lawton."

"How's business?"

Smiling that pretty smile, she said, "Very good. For once, we got the news out before it became common knowledge."

"Is Benjamin Mock back in town yet?"

"Yes. He wasn't expected back until today, but he arrived on the stage last night. He came into the office first thing this morning and actually congratulated us for printing the news."

"He wasn't mad about anything?"

"Nope. All he said was Trinidad needs a good newspaper, and he hopes we continue publishing."

"Well, I'll be d-darned."

She sold another newspaper and pocketed the pennies. Then another. "Thank you."

"I'd like to talk to you again when you get time, maybe this afternoon."

"Of course, Lawton. Anytime."

The dun horse was glad to get out of the stable, and moved along happily when Lawton mounted him and turned him

116

east out of town. He rode for an hour, at a walk, then a trot, then a slow gallop, then a walk again on the way back to the wagon camp. The horse showed a little sorefootedness. When he got to the wagon yard, Lawton gathered his bay pack horse and went looking for the blacksmith shop he'd seen on the north side. He might need the horses fast and it wouldn't do to have them sorefooted.

Instead of being big and heavily muscled, the blacksmith was short with an average build. He didn't ask Lawton's name, just trimmed the horses' feet, heated some steel shoes, fitted them and nailed them on, clinching the beveled nails where they came out of the sides of the hooves. Lawton brushed flies off the horses while the blacksmith worked. Neither horse had ever been shod, and they didn't like having their feet pounded on, but the blacksmith had been jerked around by horses before. He managed to hang onto their feet. Lawton could see there was an advantage to being short. A short man could squat under a horse easier than a tall man.

"Whew." The blacksmith wiped sweat from his forehead with a shirt sleeve after he'd let the last hoof down. "Where're these brutes from, anyway?"

"Southern New Mexico. We don't have to shoe our horses down there, just trim their feet now and then."

"Southern New Mexico? Say, you're not . . . are you the gent I read about in the paper this morning?"

"Yeah. I'm Lawton Coop."

"Well goddamn." An angry scowl came over the blacksmith's face. He threw down his rasp, shoved his cap back and put his hands on his hips. "Why'n hell didn't you say so. You're the brother of that thievin' Baylor Coop."

"Now just a damn minute. My brother is no thief."

"The hell he ain't. I say he is."

Those were fighting words. The two men stared at each other. The blacksmith carried no gun. A pistol would get in his way while he worked. Lawton's Colt was holstered at his right hand. He couldn't shoot an unarmed man. What he could do was take the gun off and fight with his fists. The man wanted a fight, was daring him to fight. If Baylor had been here he would have knocked him on his ass immediately.

Lawton started to unbuckle the gunbelt. Paused. He couldn't fight everybody, and he sure didn't want to kill this man. Finally, "How much do I owe you?"

"Ten dollars."

"That's way too much and you know it."

"Not for you it ain't."

With his left hand, Lawton took a roll of bills from his shirt pocket, and with his right hand peeled off a five and a one. "Because they were hard to shoe, I'll pay you a hell of a lot more than I'd pay otherwise. Here."

"I said ten dollars."

Mouth clamped shut, Lawton stepped close to the man. He was taller by a good two inches. Keeping his eyes locked on the blacksmith's eyes, he stepped even closer and stuffed the bills in the man's shirt pocket. He expected a reaction, a blow. He was ready for it, ready to dodge it and throw a left-hand punch himself. He had it planned; two left jabs and then a right. His eyes and the hard look on his face showed he was ready. The blacksmith didn't move. Lawton stepped back, still ready.

For a long moment the two men stared at each other. Then Lawton picked up the bridle reins and the halter rope and walked away, leading his two horses. He kept the horses between himself and the blacksmith shop until he'd covered a hundred yards, then with one backward glance he mounted the dun and rode on, breathing a sigh of relief.

He'd got away from that one without a fight. But there'd be others.

Chapter Sixteen

As he rode back to Commerce Street he wondered how much money the blacksmith had lost in the bank robbery. A robbery that Baylor Coop was accused of. Hell, that Baylor Coop had committed. He would have given anything to ask his brother about that. He was sure Baylor had an explanation. But Baylor was hiding from the law and couldn't be found.

Well, there was another man who knew all about that robbery. The bank president. Lawton had several questions to ask of him. He tied up at a hitchrail in front of the Merchants bank and went in. Mr. Mock was in his office, but another gentleman was in with him, Lawton was told. He waited, standing first on one foot and then another.

Waited. Went outside, took some deep breaths, went back in and waited.

Finally, the office door opened and a man wearing a rancher's big hat and boots came out. He even had spurs on his boots. A man of average build in good wool pants and a black vest. A neatly trimmed black beard. No range bum, this. He paused when he spotted Lawton, and the two looked each other over. Then he nodded "Mornin'," and went on past and out the door.

"Mr. Coop." It was Benjamin Mock calling, standing in

the open door of his office, smiling. "What brings you out this fine morning?"

"I'd like to talk to you a minute, Mr. Mock, if you're not too busy."

"Come in."

Lawton followed him in, sat and crossed his legs. Benjamin Mock sat behind his desk. "Mr. Mock," Lawton began, "I'd sure like to know everything about that bank robbery, the one my brother is accused of. Would you mind telling me exactly what happened?"

The banker had shaved just that morning, and still smelled of bay rum. He spread his hands and shrugged. "I believe I told you before. There's no more to tell. I'd had company and they had just left. I was getting ready for bed when Baylor Coop knocked on the door. Mrs. Willis opened the door and Baylor Coop came in with a revolver pointed right at me. He forced me under threat of immediate death to accompany him to the bank and open the safe. He knew somehow that only I can open the safe. He took all the money, put it in a gunny sack and was ready to leave when Sheriff Spates came in. Baylor Coop fired one shot from his revolver and Sheriff Spates fell dead. I heard hoofbeats as Mr. Coop left town on a gallop. That's all there is to it."

"It was easy, wasn't it? Robbing the bank was a simple and easy thing to do."

"Yes, but . . . what can I do? I considered leaving the key with the sheriff during the night, but as yet I haven't done that. Perhaps I will in the future."

"You said Mrs. Willis opened the door when Baylor knocked?"

"She did. She has been keeping house for me since Orville Jackson died. And yes, she did see and recognize Baylor Coop. In fact, it was she who went for the sheriff."

Lawton mulled that over and realized he was getting nowhere. He changed the subject. "You read in the newspaper about the shooting at the Watkins homestead. I

120

was wondering . . . Mrs. Watkins said they tried to buy the land from you and you wouldn't sell."

The banker opened a box of cigars, offered one to Lawton, took one himself after Lawton shook his head. "We're not opening up the entire Maxwell grant for sale. Mr. Springs is one of the principal stockholders in the Maxwell Land Company, and he is running some cattle on this end of the grant. Furthermore, he is planning to import more cattle from Texas. The, uh, Watkins place is along Kettle Creek, a source of water for livestock."

He used a small silver knife to cut off the end of his cigar, lit it with a wooden match and blew a cloud of smoke at the ceiling. "Now, I know what you're thinking. It's what a lot of folks are thinking. What's fifty acres out of a million and five hundred thousand acres. But being a cattleman yourself, you ought to understand. Sell them fifty acres and they'll fence it off. Then somebody else will want fifty acres, and somebody else. Within a few years the whole creek would be fenced off."

Nodding, Lawton had to agree. This was another line of questioning that was getting nowhere. He tried a different angle.

"The six hundred acres my brother bought, is it in the way of a bigger cattle operation?"

The banker took another drag on his cigar and blew another cloud of smoke. "In the first place, Baylor Coop did not buy any land. He merely picked a spot and built a cabin on it. We have had to, uh, discourage a number of squatters, and he was just one of them. In the second place, suppose we did sell him six hundred acres. Mr. Springs would have to build a fence around it. Otherwise any cattle owned by Baylor Coop would graze free on Mr. Springs's range. It would have been a difficult situation."

Another dead end. Lawton had only one more question: "I, uh, saw a curious hole in the ground on the land my brother claimed, and Thomas Watkins said he has seen holes like it. What are they?"

A puzzled look came over the banker's face. "Holes? What kind of holes?"

"About as big around as a man's fist with black dust around them."

"Gopher holes? Uh, Mr. Coop, being a stranger in this part of the country, you perhaps aren't familiar with the small pocket gophers that are so common. They dig holes about that size."

"They look like they were dug with an auger of some kind."

Shaking his head, Benjamin Mock said, "You've got me there. I have no idea what you're talking about."

That was that. No use asking more questions. Lawton felt defeated as he stood and put on his hat. "Well, thanks for your time, Mr. Mock."

He rode at a slow walk back to the wagon camp, deep in thought, seeing nothing, hearing nothing. The dun horse had its head up, ears twitching, catching every sound and every sight. At the stables, he offsaddled, watered his horses at a steel tank and tied them to a hay manger. The boy, Thomas Watkins, was raking manure out of an empty stall.

"How's your dad?" Lawton asked.

"He doesn't hurt as much today, but he has to carry his arm in a sling. I got a job cleaning up these stables until we can go back home."

"You're going back then?"

"Yeah. Mr. Mock, the banker, came to see us this mornin' and told us we could stay there till we harvest our crops, then we'll have to leave."

"He said that?"

"Yeah. He told us why he couldn't sell us fifty acres, and I reckon we can't blame 'im much. He didn't have nothin' to do with them gunslingers shootin' at us. It was some of the other stockholders. He didn't have to come and see us. He's a real nice feller."

"Sure," Lawton muttered as he walked away, "he's a real nice feller."

The Trinchera Eatery was packed, and the counterman didn't have time to talk. That was fine with Lawton. But another customer did. "Say, are you . . . ?"

"Yeah, that's me."

The man looked quickly away, and Lawton realized he'd been gruff, unsociable. He thought about apologizing. Not everyone in Trinidad hated the Coops. But he didn't apologize.

James C. Gordon was alone in the newspaper building, sitting at the desk, writing with a lead pencil. He looked up through his half-lens glasses when Lawton entered, said, "Hello, Mr. Coop. Fine day."

"I'm sorry to bother you, Mr. Gordon. I'd like to ask you about something. But I can come back some other time."

The newspaperman put his pencil down, turned in his chair and peered at Lawton over the glasses. "We went to press early this morning, and sold out by mid-morning. Annie finally went home to get some rest, but I can spare some time."

Lawton perched on the stool. "I don't have anything very important to ask about. I'm just kind of fishing, you might say, grabbing at anything."

"I can imagine how you feel."

"Baylor was tricked into coming to town the day he was arrested, and he busted out of jail. How did he do that? Bust out, I mean."

"He overpowered the deputy, William Core, locked him in his own cell and ran. As I understand it, his horse was being kept in the deputy's pen on the west side, and Baylor Coop just went there, retrieved his horse and rode away."

"Easy, huh?"

A semblance of a smile appeared on Gordon's serious

123

face. "Deputy Core was a little embarrassed."

"Did, uh, did County Clerk Orville Jackson die before or after Baylor was arrested?"

"The same night. Is that important?"

"Oh, I don't know." Lawton looked down at his boots. "It could be. I don't know." Looking up again, he said, "According to Mrs. Willis, Baylor went to Jackson's house to talk to him once. Only reason is Jackson was too sick to go to his office that day and Baylor wanted to see him bad enough to bother him at home."

"Orville Jackson did occasionally stay at home."

"What Baylor wanted to see him about was Baylor had bought that six hundred acres, but the county's record of the sale had disappeared."

"That's what Annie believes."

"Yeah." He looked down at his boots again, then, "Doesn't it seem strange to you, Mr. Gordon, that a deed to some land disappeared from the county clerk's office and soon after that the county clerk died?"

"Hmm. Well, Orville Jackson was a very sick man. We all expected him to pass on any day."

"Yeah. Well." He stood. "Tell me something, Mr. Gordon, what do you think of my brother? Do you think he did everything he's accused of?"

Taking off his glasses and wiping them carefully with a handkerchief, the newspaperman pondered the questions. "As a journalist, I have a habit of being entirely objective. Nobody is guilty until proven guilty. The evidence against Baylor Coop is, to put it mildly, overwhelming. I'm sure a trial jury would find him guilty in a minute. But . . ." He paused, then went on, "Annie was quite taken with Baylor Coop, and she is not a foolish, stupid child. She was engaged to a young man in Illinoi before we came out here. It didn't turn out well. I'm sure she would not make that mistake again."

Lawton had to chuckle. "Annie is a fine young lady." He turned to go.

"I haven't been much help, have I?"

"Aw, who knows. Any little piece of information I can pick up might help."

"Good luck to you, Mr. Coop."

"Lawton. Call me Lawton. Or Law. My dad was Mr. Coop."

That got another almost-smile from James C. Gordon.

On his way to the new courthouse, he walked past the Merchants Hotel, a two-story clapboard building with a large plate glass window. He looked in as he passed, saw a lobby with a carpet, a few chairs and a desk. If he hadn't had horses to care for, he'd have taken a room in the hotel. A man could take a bath in there. He needed a bath. He went on to the courthouse.

Mrs. Margaret Tuders was standing at the counter in the county clerk's office, talking to a Mexican couple. The couple, middle-aged, work-worn, could speak very little English, but the county clerk assured them with a combination of Spanish and English that they had legal title to some land. When she pointed east, Lawton guessed that the land in question was east of town and not part of the Maxwell grant.

Nodding with a broad smile, the man said, "Gracias, Señora," took his wife by the arm and left.

But the county clerk was exasperated. "You'd think since they live in an English-speaking country, that they would learn the language."

He felt like reminding her that the Mexicans were here first, but he didn't want to argue. Instead, he asked about land transactions on the Maxwell grant. "They did sell some land, didn't they?"

"Oh yes. They sold quite a few parcels in this county, and I hear they've sold more in New Mexico Territory. Why do you ask?"

"I'm just curious."

"Well, I have a lot of paperwork to do, and I don't have

125

time to answer questions just to satisfy everybody's curiosity."

"Uh, I don't mean to be disrespectful, Mrs. Tuders, but I believe records of land transactions are public."

"Yes, they are. However, you will have to search for yourself. One moment." She went to the wooden cabinet, pulled out a thick sheaf of papers. Placing them on the counter in front of Lawton, she said, "You can look all you want to." She went to her desk.

He looked. It meant nothing to him. Section 19, township 12 south, range 68 west of the 6th P.M. . . . He concentrated on names. Hawthorn, Beakley, Roberts . . .

"Excuse me, I'm sorry to bother you, but would you tell me, are these people mostly homesteaders who bought their land?"

"Yes. Nearly all of them. If they hadn't already been there they would have bought land elsewhere for less money."

"Is that right?" He turned pages, read more names.

"Be careful you don't get those out of order. I have them arranged so I can find anything immediately."

It occurred to him that it would be easy to steal some of the sheets. Just wait until the clerk wasn't looking and quietly fold them up and put them in his pocket. That's what happened to the deed to Baylor's six hundred acres. He said, "I'll be careful."

Willhoit, Gables, Spates.

Spates?

He looked closer. William S. Spates.

"Excuse me again, ma'am, but is this the William S. Spates who was sheriff here?"

"Yes, it is. Was."

"Is this land he bought . . . I'm not a land surveyor as you might guess, and these legal descriptions mean nothing to me, but would you mind telling me the approximate whereabouts of this parcel?"

She came back to the counter and took the sheet from his

126

hands. "It's, uh, I'd say about, oh, ten miles southwest of the town limits."

"Yeah? It says a hundred acres."

"Yes. One hundred acres."

"And he bought this from the Maxwell Land Company?"

"That's what it says. Right here."

"Uh-huh. That's interesting. Thank you, Mrs. Tuders, you've been real nice." He thought he saw her face soften a little.

That night Lawton Coop came within an inch of being shot to death.

Chapter Seventeen

The bed in his rented cabin looked mighty inviting with its soft springs and mattress. Better than a bed on the floor. But possibly dangerous. He slept on the floor in his own bedroll with the spring bed between him and the door. At first he couldn't sleep, thinking of Mary and the baby. How much longer before the baby was born? Would she have enough warning to get to White Lake and an experienced midwife, or would his mother have to deliver the baby? More important, would he be there? He had an urge to get up, do something, finish this job. But what could he do at night? For that matter, what would he do in the morning? And Baylor. If Baylor came back he could answer a lot of questions. But Baylor's life wouldn't be worth a plugged nickel in southern Colorado Territory. He would be a fool to come back.

Finally he dozed.

It was a dream. Lawton and Baylor were sitting cross-legged on the ground, talking. Their horses were standing hobbled a few yards away. They were trying to estimate how many beeves they would have to sell to pay off the note at the bank in Roswell. Lawton was scratching some figures in the dirt when Baylor suddenly stiffened, and said quietly, "Don't move, Law. Sit mighty still." Lawton suspected what the danger was and didn't move. Baylor got up slowly, drew his six-gun, stepped to one side, aimed and fired.

The rattlesnake behind Lawton was as long as a man's arm and almost as big around. It was writhing as it died, its head shattered by a .44 slug.

"Good shot, Bay."

"You have to be careful, Law." Baylor's face began to dissolve in the dream. "Be careful, be careful . . . Look out, Law."

He awoke with a snort and grabbed for the Colt under the blanket. At the same instant the door crashed open and a shotgun boomed.

The explosion of the 16-gauge was so loud that he thought the whole cabin had blown up. He was trying to gather his senses when the second barrel boomed. Something stung the left side of his neck, and the noise had his brain whirling for a second.

But only for a second. He aimed at a dim figure in the dark doorway and squeezed off a shot. Fanning the hammer with the edge of his left hand, he fired twice more. The whole world was one big explosion after another. The figure disappeared. A man's voice said, "Let's go."

Then it was quiet.

He stayed where he was on the floor, eyes straining, watching the doorway, ready to shoot again. Listening. Quiet. His ears were ringing from the noise.

The whole thing had happened in a matter of seconds. He couldn't believe he was still alive. He waited.

Well, he couldn't just stay there on the floor. Had to get up. Best way to do it, he figured, was to jump up and get to the wall next to the door. Flatten himself against the wall. Fast.

Do it.

Sweeping the blanket and tarp off with his left hand, he jumped up, stumbled over the tarp, straightened up and took three long swift steps to the wall. He stood with his back to the wall next to the door. The Colt was in his right hand. The hammer was back.

Still quiet. Not a sound. He waited.

Come on, you sonsofbitches, he muttered under his breath. Try that again.

They wouldn't try it again. They'd fired both barrels into the bed and gone.

He stood there in his sock feet and finally convinced himself that the danger was over. Moving slowly, wishing he had his boots on, he stepped to the door, looked out into the black night. He stepped through the door. He stumbled over something, something soft.

Eyes straining again, he tried to see what it was. Couldn't make it out. He squatted and touched it, then drew his hand back as if he'd touched something vile. It was a man. The man wasn't moving.

"Jumping Jehosaphat," he muttered.

Lights came on in two of the cabins. Dim lamplights. A light came on in the owner's cabin. Lawton stood still and watched as the light came outside with a man behind it.

"Hey. What's going on? Hey."

"Over here," Lawton yelled. "They're gone now. Bring the light over here."

The light approached, bobbing as the man walked. "Where?"

"Over here."

Then the lantern was held up, illuminating Lawton's face. "What the holy hell happened?"

"They tried to kill me in my sleep. Watch where you step. One of them is down."

The lantern was lowered. "Jesus Christ. Is he . . . ?"

"He ain't moving."

"What the holy hell . . . ?"

Two more lights approached, lamps with glass chimneys. "Who done all the shootin'?"

"Did somebody get shot?"

Within two minutes, five men were gathered around the body. The dead man was lying on his back, eyes and mouth open. He wore flat-heeled boots, and a wide-brim hat was on the ground near his head. "Anybody know 'im?"

"I seen 'im just last night. In the Raton saloon. Him and some others."

"Know his name?"

"Naw." Another lamp was held up to Lawton's face. "Did you shoot 'im, mister?"

"Yeah." Lawton let the hammer down on the Colt, holstered it and stepped inside his rented cabin. He groped his way to the lamp table, found some matches and lit the lamp. "Look here."

They all squeezed in, and "Awwed" at the two holes in the bed, both the size of a man's hand. "How'n holy hell'd they miss you?"

"I was sleeping on the floor over there."

"You musta knowed they was comin'. Say, ain't you . . . ?"

"Yeah."

"Man, somebody sure wants your hide."

"Yeah."

"You're bleedin'. You been shot yourself?"

He wiped a hand across the left side of his neck. The hand came away bloody.

"You better go see the doc, mister."

"Yeah."

It took a swab of alcohol, a scalpel and a pair of tweezers to get two buckshot pellets out of Lawton's neck. Lawton lay on his side with his shirt off and gritted his teeth to hold back a groan while Doctor Hiram Bromley worked on him.

Another swab of alcohol, and it was over. "It will bleed for a while, but it will heal nicely. That is, if you keep it clean. How did you get hit by two stray pellets?"

"Must have ricocheted off the bed springs. That's the only

131

explanation I can think of."

"I've got some gum here that will hold a bandage over the wound."

He buttoned his shirt and tucked the tail of it in his pants. "How much do I owe you?"

"Oh, make it two dollars."

Walking back to the wagon yard, his neck was sore to the touch and turning his head was something he did slowly and carefully. He was sure he knew who tried to kill him. He didn't know their names, but he knew where they came from. While he was feeding his horses, Sheriff Horace Willard walked up. Lawton told him what had happened. The lawman talked to the camp owner next, then two of the renters, went inside Lawton's rented cabin, came back.

He said, "There's no doubt in my mind they're from the Maxwell outfit. And I can guess why they tried to blow you in two with a scattergun."

"It's easy to figure," Lawton said, forking hay into the manger. "They wanted revenge."

"Yup. You shot one of their pals off his horse out there on Kettle Creek, and they got to boozin' it up in El Raton and decided to get even."

"What are you gonna do about it?"

Pushing his hat back and scratching his head, Willard drawled, "What can I do? I found two men who saw that jasper in the Raton, but the men he was drinkin' with are long gone. Whoever they are, they pulled their freight right after the shootin'."

"Somebody knows who they are."

"Sure, everybody knows who they are. Maybe nobody knows their names, but everybody knows they work for the Maxwell."

"Where is the Maxwell ranch headquarters?"

"Southwest, on a creek that's called, uh, Squaw Creek, I think. I went down there once a couple months ago, and they had me surrounded two minutes after I rode up to the house.

132

They laughed at me and made damn sure I understood that they were in Colfax County, Territory of New Mexico. Out of my jurisdiction."

"The men who surrounded you, would you recognize them if they came to Trinidad?"

"Sure. Howard Rowe was one of them. He manages the outfit. But I can't arrest him because I've got nothing on him. I can't arrest any of them for that matter. Nobody can identify them as the shooters. Besides, the sheriff down there told me men come and go on that outfit."

"How far is the headquarters?"

"About twenty miles. Maybe twenty-five. Why, you're not going down there?"

"Naw. That wouldn't accomplish anything. Have you seen Howard Rowe in town lately?"

"Yeah. Seen 'im yesterday. I think he's stayin' over at the hotel for a few days."

"What's he look like?"

"Like a cowman. He's got a beard, a black one, but he keeps it sheared. About your size."

"I saw him in the bank yesterday. I think I'll go over to the hotel and introduce myself."

"You're not gonna start any more shootin', are you?"

Howard Rowe wasn't in his room at the hotel. He wasn't in the hotel's restaurant. The more Lawton thought about the shooting and the attack on the Watkinses, the angrier he got. He went back out on the sidewalk and saw Howard Rowe coming. He stepped in front of him.

"You're Howard Rowe." It came out as an accusation.

"That's right, I am."

"You know who I am."

"Sure, I know who you are. What do you want?"

"I want to know why some of your hired men tried to kill me last night, and I want to know why your hired men shot

133

Ephram Watkins."

"What are you talking about?"

"You know what I'm talking about, and you can name the men I'm talking about."

The ranch manager pulled his hat down tighter and scowled. "Are you accusing me of hiring killers?"

"That's right."

For a minute, neither man spoke. They stood on the sidewalk, face to face, both carrying six-guns in holsters on their right hips. Lawton had always prided himself in never having started a fight. But he'd never been held and beaten before, nor shot at while he lay asleep. He'd never felt so frustrated. Everything that had happened was started by someone else. This man was responsible for at least part of it. Now he wanted to start something. He wanted to hit back at somebody. He stood straddle-legged, ready.

Finally, the bearded man spoke. "You're the brother of a man who robbed a bank and killed a sheriff, and you're mad at the town and looking for a chance to shoot somebody. Why the hell are you picking on me?"

"Because you hire gunslingers, the kind of men who'll shoot their own mothers for enough money. Everyone knows that. Your men shoot and run back across the New Mexico border where the sheriff can't get at them."

"I run a cow outfit and I hire cowboys."

"Huh-uh. They might look like cowboys to some people, but not to me. And not to you either. They're not staying around here, so they have to be staying on your so-called cow outfit."

Another stare-down. Then, "You're looking for a fight, ain't you, Coop."

"Yeah. I'm tired of this whole mess. Some men around here smell like an outhouse, and you're one of them."

"Take some advice, Coop. Go back to where you come from. You're not gonna do any good here." With that, Howard Rowe stepped around Lawton and went into the hotel.

Lawton stood there, head down. Stood there for a long moment. He was tense, ready for a fight, and it took a while to force himself to relax. Again he'd risked his life for nothing—without accomplishing one damned thing. He'd acted out of anger and frustration. It wasn't the sort of thing a sensible man would do. Get your wits about you, Lawton Coop, he muttered under his breath. Go somewhere and think this over.

The counterman was busy, but he couldn't contain his curiosity. "Heard what happened. You're givin' this town almost as much to talk about as your brother did." His eyes were fixed on the white bandage. "How'd they hit you in the neck without killin' you?"

Lawton grumbled. "I'm a tough bird. Almost as tough as this boar gut you're feeding everybody this morning."

Outside he realized he'd been cranky. The bacon wasn't that bad. He had to calm himself. Get on a horse. That always helped.

Chapter Eighteen

It took a few miles for the dun horse to realize the rocks didn't hurt his feet anymore, and Lawton liked the sound of steel on the rocks. He rode northwest, north of the Picketwire, and reined up when he saw smoke on the other side of a hill ahead. Thinking of a grass or timber fire, he rode at a gallop toward it. As soon as he topped the hill he saw the smoke was coming from a steam engine that ran a sawmill. Stopping there, he looked down, saw men working, heard the high whine of the blade, saw a man shoveling coal into the firebox under the steam boiler. Coal? Yeah, that's what it was. He'd heard of coal, even seen some once on a trip to Santa Fe. But he'd never handled it. It made a good fire, he'd heard.

After a while, he turned his horse around and rode off the hill in the opposite direction. If he'd gone down there to be sociable, he might have had to fight somebody. He'd had enough of that.

He found a grassy spot near a narrow stream, dismounted, dropped the reins and sat on the ground under a juniper. The dun horse went after the high country grass as if it was the best roughage he'd ever tasted. A pleasant spot. Cool, quiet. He enjoyed the sound of the creek and the sound of his horse cropping the grass. A man could calm his nerves here. Do some thinking.

As usual his thoughts went to Mary, his mother, Baylor. He fingered the sore spot on the side of his neck and recalled the last time Baylor had left home. Lawton had talked to him, told him he didn't need to go. The ranch could support two families, and just because he'd taken a wife didn't mean there wasn't room for everybody. Baylor had chuckled. He wasn't leaving because of Mary. Hell, he liked Mary. She was a fine woman. A man couldn't ask for a better sister-in-law. No, he just wanted to see more of the country. Colorado sounded good. Men were getting rich digging up gold. He'd punched Lawton playfully on the shoulder. "I'm glad you got married, Law. Somebody around here has to raise a family. Hell, who knows, one of these days I might find the right woman myself. I'm not looking yet, but, hell, who knows."

That's one thing Baylor didn't have to look for, a woman. They looked for him. With his dark curly hair and handsome grin, he could have taken his pick of the young women within a hundred miles of the Circle C. But he wasn't about to let some girl get a loop around him. Or was he?

Come to think of it, Annie Gordon had him begging. The way she told it, she liked him very much until he got into a saloon killing. Then he'd had to beg to get her interested in him again. She hadn't called it begging, but that's what it was. And no wonder. She could have any man begging.

Yep, Lawton chuckled to himself, old Bay done went and got wide-eyed and ring-tailed over a girl.

But—the chuckle disappeared—too bad it turned out the way it did.

Still another unpleasant thought came to his mind after he mounted and headed back for town: he was the older brother, and, yeah, he had to admit to himself that he did bully Baylor at times. Until Baylor outgrew him. He'd thought about it before, and it always made him feel guilty. He wished he hadn't done that.

The twin holes in the bed hadn't been patched and the splintered doorjamb hadn't been fixed. Lawton went to the camp owner and asked for another cabin. "Why?" the owner said. "If I put somebody else in that cabin they might draw fire intended for you. Nope, you either stay in that one or take your horses and yourself out of here."

He didn't want to argue. He shrugged and walked away. He'd seen a livery barn on the south side and he could maybe put his horses up there and stay in the hotel. Maybe not. The livery owner might hate the Coop family. He'd have to stay here.

It was well past noon, but he'd try the Trinchera Eatery anyway. A piece of bread, anything, would be better than nothing. Walking past the Las Animas Gazette, he glanced through the open door and saw Annie sitting at the desk. She saw him. He waved. She jumped up and hurried to the door.

"Oh, Lawton," she called. He turned. "Lawton, could I talk to you a minute?"

"Sure, Annie."

"Come in. I've got some coffee on." Then she saw the bandage on his neck. "Oh my. Is that serious?"

"Naw." He entered the building behind her and removed his hat. She went to a small pot-bellied stove with a flat top in a far corner of the room, picked up a galvanized coffeepot and poured a china cup full. "Sit here at the desk, Lawton." He sat and sipped the coffee. "Have you had dinner? I've got some bread and apple butter."

"No, I haven't, and that sounds good."

She opened a desk drawer and took out a loaf of bread wrapped in newsprint and a jar of apple butter. He sliced the bread with a long knife she'd produced and ate. "Good. Real good."

"I'd like to ask you about the shooting last night. The story is old stuff by now, but maybe you can give me some details that are not common knowledge."

"Sure." He told her everything.

138

"And you think they were seeking revenge because you helped the Watkins family defend their homestead?"

"Yeah. That's what I think."

She sighed. "Well, that's not news anymore, but we'll print it in the next edition. Do you mind if I quote you as saying they were seeking revenge? That will give me something, a lead."

"A lead?"

"Yes. Something to lead off with. The first paragraph."

"Oh."

"What will you do now, Lawton?"

Now it was his turn to sigh. "What I'd like to do is question that housekeeper, Mrs. Willis, but I reckon that's hopeless."

"I'll talk to her again. Maybe, if I talk to her alone, if I'm persuasive enough, she'll be willing to talk to you. I'll try. When do you want to do it?"

"As soon as possible. Right now, if that's possible."

"She'll be at Mr. Mock's house now, but . . . well, we can try."

He hung back when Annie knocked on the door. The house was adobe with a red tile roof. He guessed there were four rooms. Maybe five. Whoever had built it had been careful not to trample the clump grass that grew around the house and to leave the piñon trees. A wooden table and four chairs sat next to a tree in the front yard.

"Annie Gordon." Mrs. Willis was surprised to see her. "What brings you here?"

"Mrs. Willis," Annie began, "I know I'm imposing on you, coming here, but this is very important. Mr. Coop would like to ask you about Orville Jackson's death."

She saw Lawton then, standing in the front yard. "I have no wish to speak with Mr. Coop."

"Please, Mrs. Willis. Lawton Coop is an honest and honorable man. He owns one of the biggest cattle ranches in

139

New Mexico Territory. He is only trying to find out how his brother got into so much trouble."

"There was another shooting last night and he was right in the middle of it."

"Yes. And you know why, don't you? It was because he helped an honest, hard-working family defend their homestead."

"Yes. I read about that in the newspaper." Did she soften a little? "According to your newspaper, the Watkinses might all have been murdered if it wasn't for Lawton Coop."

"Won't you speak to him, Mrs. Willis?"

"Well, I can't allow you in the house. This house belongs to Mr. Mock, and I'm not at liberty to invite anybody in."

"How about over there?" Annie nodded toward the table and chairs.

"Well."

"Only for a few minutes."

She came out, carefully closing the door behind her. Lawton approached, touched his hat brim. "I appreciate this, Mrs. Willis. I won't take much of your time, I promise."

"Well." She sat in one of the chairs. Annie and Lawton occupied two others.

"What I'm curious about is the death of Orville Jackson." Before she could say anything, he added, "I know he was a lunger and a very sick man. But . . . it's probably just one of those things, I mean, that he died the night my brother was arrested. Were you there when he died?"

"Yes," she said with a hint of irritation. "I was there all night. I was staying there at the time."

"Would you mind telling me exactly what happened? Was anybody else there?"

"Mr. Jackson come home around noon that day, feeling very poorly. He went right to bed, but later he got up and talked for a minute to Baylor Coop and ate some bean soup and went back to bed. Sheriff Spates came calling that evening, after Mr. Jackson had retired for the night."

140

"Sheriff Spates?"

"He said he had some important business to discuss, something that couldn't wait. I opened the bedroom door and asked Mr. Jackson if he wanted to talk to the sheriff and he said to show the sheriff in."

"Umm. Well. I don't suppose you know what they talked about."

"Certainly not. I am not in the habit of listening at keyholes."

"Oh, sure. I didn't mean that. What I mean is, was the bedroom door closed?"

"Yes, it was. Young man, I have work to do."

"Just another minute, Mrs. Willis. Uh, how long was the sheriff there?"

"Only a short time."

"And did you see Orville Jackson alive after the sheriff left?"

"No, I did not."

"Oh? You didn't see him alive again?"

"But I heard him."

"You heard him?"

"Yes. He had another of his coughing fits."

"After the sheriff left?"

"Yes. I must get back to my work."

"One more question. When did you find out he was dead?"

"The next morning. I went in to awaken him and found him cold and stiff. He died some time during the night."

"What did he look like? I mean, uh, was he in bed, or . . . ?"

"He was in bed. He had coughed blood as usual."

"Oh. Hmm. Well." Lawton could think of no more questions. "I'm much obliged, Mrs. Willis."

Walking back to the Gazette, Lawton was quiet, deep in thought. It was the girl who spoke first. "I don't suppose it means anything, but I hadn't heard about Baylor and the sheriff visiting Orville Jackson the night he died."

"First Baylor and then the sheriff. Nobody mentioned that before, huh?"

"If they did, I didn't hear about it, and I make it a point to hear about everything."

"It doesn't seem to be a secret."

"No. Apparently, you're the only one who asked whether he had any visitors."

"I reckon it doesn't make any difference."

"No, I can't see any significance in it. Orville Jackson died of tuberculosis as everyone knew he would."

At the Gazette door, she paused. "Would you care to come in, Lawton? I'll put the coffeepot back on the stove."

"No, uh . . ." He rubbed his jaw. "I've got to do something. I don't know what. I've asked all the questions I can think of. I don't know of anybody else to question. But I've got to do something."

"Come in, Lawton, and let's put the coffee on."

He followed her inside. James C. Gordon was setting type in the back of the room. He looked over his glasses and nodded a greeting. Lawton nodded back. "Sit in the chair, Lawton. I'll be back in a minute."

He sat and tried to think while she busied herself with the coffeepot. When she returned, she perched on the stool, facing him. "I understand how you feel, Lawton. I feel the same way. There are things we don't know. It's frustrating."

"Yeah. Did you know Sheriff Spates bought a hundred acres from the land company, just west of town a ways?"

"Yes, I knew that. I make a habit of checking public records now and then in case there's news in them."

"Does that strike you as strange? They won't sell to the nesters who've been there all along, but they'll sell to the sheriff."

"It's odd. They also sold a hundred acres to Howard Rowe."

"They did? I didn't see that. I quit looking, I reckon, when I came across Sheriff Spates's name." Lawton grinned a wry grin. "If I had to make a living as a detective, I'd starve."

They were silent, both in a dark mood. Lawton fingered the bandage on his neck. When the coffeepot boiled, she got up and poured two cups, came back. They sipped hot black coffee. Then she stood.

"I can't let Dad do all the work. We've got some advertising copy to set. You stay here and finish your coffee."

"No, I, uh. Thanks just the same, but, uh, tell me something, did Sheriff Spates leave a widow?"

"No. He lived alone. He had a two-room house on the north end."

"Is the house still empty?"

"Yes, it is. I walked past there just a few days ago, and it looked vacant."

"Would you tell me how to find it?"

"Sure. It's easy to find. Why?"

Shrugging, he answered, "Oh, I don't know. I'm just curious."

He finished his coffee, thanked the girl and went back to the wagon camp. He would have to wait until after dark, but when dark came he knew what he was going to do. It was useless, but he had to do something. It was also illegal as hell, and he could be shot.

But he was going to have a look inside the house where the late Sheriff William S. Spates had lived.

Chapter Nineteen

Dogs barked and a mule brayed. The night was a black one with a new moon, which meant no moon at all. He had located the house before dark so he believed he could go right to it. It sat on an acre-sized lot surrounded with weeds, an indication that the ground had once been plowed. The nearest neighbor was in the next block. So was the nearest dog. It was barking, but its owner was used to hearing it and paid it no mind. Dogs were barking across town at each other.

The house was nothing more than a big dark blob in front of him as he approached. Groping, he found the front door. Locked with a big padlock. Still groping, he made his way around the house to the back door. Another padlock. He remembered seeing a boarded-up window near the back door, and he found it, got hold of a board with his fingers and pulled. Nailed tight. A tool of any kind would help, but he had none. He pulled again, strained, gritted his teeth, grunted and pulled. A nail creaked. Strained again. Another creak.

Straining until he thought his back would break, he pulled one end of a board loose, then quickly pried off the other end. The dog in the next block was furious now. It knew something illicit was going on. The back door of that house opened and a man came out, carrying a lantern. Lawton stood perfectly still against the sheriff's house as the man walked around his back yard, trying to figure out what the dog was excited about. Finally, he went inside.

All right, so he had one board off, but that left an opening of only six inches. He had to pull off more boards. And try to be quiet. He got hold of a board and pulled, strained, grunted. It splintered and split. Got another hold, pulled. Nails creaked. The board came free. The dog was still barking, but no one was paying any attention. Got hold of another board, pulled, grunted.

Now he had three boards off, leaving a gap of about eighteen inches. Not quite enough. The next board was nailed tighter. Wouldn't give at all. Lawton put one foot against the wall for leverage and pulled with all his strength. He gritted his teeth and pulled. Grunted. The board cracked and split down the middle.

Hell. Noisy enough to alert the whole town.

He squatted under the window and listened, expecting to hear someone coming to investigate. Listened for several long minutes. All he heard was the dog barking. Straightening, he discovered he had a gap of about twenty inches in the window. Maybe he could squeeze through that. He'd try.

He hooked his fingers over the windowsill and pulled himself up. Kicking and squirming, he got his head and shoulders through. It was even darker inside than it was outside, and he had no idea what was under the window. He kicked and squirmed some more and got his legs horizontal with the ground. In as far as his waist now. Stopped.

Damn belt buckle. Caught on something. The buckle on his gun belt.

Grunting with the exertion, he managed to turn on his left side and pull himself in a little farther. Now the gun belt was free. Sliding in the rest of the way should be easy.

Not so easy. Something was under the window. His fingers explored, and he believed it was a chair. While he was groping, trying to push the chair out of the way, he slipped and fell inside. He lit on his hands and turned a somersault. The chair was knocked over with a crash and his boots hit the floor with a double thump. The Colt six-shooter fell out of its holster and clattered to the floor too.

"God damn."

The first thing he did after he picked himself up was find the pistol. It took both hands, but he found it and put it back in its holster. Then he poked his head through the window and took a long look all around outside and at the house in the next block. Only the dog seemed to care. Turning his head so far made the wound on his neck sting. Hell with that.

Now. Had to have a light. But not so close to the window. He groped, found a table and another chair, and made his way across the room to another wall. There, he pulled a sulphur match out of a shirt pocket and struck it with a thumbnail. It was a kitchen, all right. A table and some chairs, a sheepherder's stove near the other wall with a stovepipe going up through the ceiling. The match burned his fingers. He dropped it and struck another. Two wooden boxes were nailed to a wall for a cabinet. A short-handled pump was mounted over a tin sink. There was a drain hole in the sink and a rubber tube under the sink to carry drain water outside.

Striking matches to light his way, he went through a door into the other room. There was a narrow bed with blankets, wrinkled and dirty. Clothes hung from nails in the wall. A pair of boots was on the floor at the end of the bed. A long wooden box with a closed lid lay along the far wall. Uh-huh, he said under his breath, that would be the place to put anything important. He went to it, found a padlock. Struck another match. The padlock was open. He squatted on his heels and raised the lid. Clothes, papers, an old Bible.

Papers? Papers tell tales.

He wished he had a lamp. On second thought a lamp would put out too much light, and could be seen from

146

outside. But, damn, it was hard to read by matchlight. Let's see, a letter. He unfolded it.

"Deer Bill . . ." He couldn't make out the rest of it by matchlight. There was an envelope addressed to Mr. William S. Spates, postmarked Kansas City, Missouri. Nothing in it. Another envelope also addressed to William S. Spates. He opened it and took out another folded letter. Whoever wrote this one was a better speller. "Dear William . . ." It was none of his business. More envelopes, more letters. An envelope with the return address of Amarillo, Texas, from Franklin C. Spates. Probably a brother.

He had a small pile of matchsticks on the floor now, and not very many matches left. But there were a few more papers. An envelope from Pueblo, Territory of Colorado with something printed in the upper left-hand corner. Not written, but printed. Let's see.

He struck another match. First National Bank of Pueblo. Hmm. The envelope was empty.

There were some clothes, two blankets and more old letters. That was all. When another match burned his fingers, he dropped it and closed the lid on the box. Standing, he struck a match and took a longer look around the room. No guns on the walls, nothing of value anywhere. No doubt somebody had been there before him. Somebody had opened the lock on the wooden box. Opened it or broke it?

He squatted again and held a match close to the lock. Broken. Pried apart. Damn. Hell. Goddamn. If there was ever anything interesting in that box, somebody had beat him to it. Might as well go.

Working his way with his hands, he went back to the kitchen and collided with the table. Only a couple of matches left. He struck one and saw a tin plate, a cup and a knife and fork on the table beside a kerosene lamp. A pile of newspapers was near the stove, no doubt to build a fire with.

147

That match burned its way down to his fingers, and he struck the last one, held it up to the makeshift cabinet. Another plate and cup, a small bottle of laudanum. The sheriff must have been bothered with headaches. A bottle with mercury written in lead pencil across the label. What was that for? An airtight can of tomatoes and another of peaches. He had to drop the match. There were probably more matches in the house somewhere, but he didn't know where to look. To feel, rather. He'd been in there long enough anyway. Time to go.

There was only one way to get out and that was the way he'd come in. This time he hoped to make it easier on himself by standing on a chair to get started through the window. It was easier, but falling outside was not. The ground was just as hard as the floor had been. Again, he landed on his hands, head down, and turned a somersault. This time, the Colt stayed where it belonged. The dog was furious again, and Lawton wasted no time getting up and getting away from the house, walking rapidly back to the dark street.

Thank heavens for the darkness. Even if somebody came to investigate, they wouldn't see him in the dark. Walking down the dirt street, he was relieved at being safely out of the house but disappointed that he hadn't found anything interesting. Well, he really hadn't expected to come across any iron-clad proof of anything anyhow. It had been just a desperate try. What was he going to try next? Hell, he didn't know. Something, but he didn't know what.

The hoofbeats of a horse and the rattling of trace chains told him a buggy was coming toward him. He stepped aside. The man in the buggy didn't see him at first, but the horse did. It snorted and veered wide around him.

"What the goddamn hell's the matter with you? Oh." The man saw Lawton standing in the dark then.

"Evening," Lawton said, trying to sound pleasant.

"Evenin'."

Better not cuss that horse too much, Lawton mused. You're gonna need that horse's eyes to find your way home.

At the wagon camp, he realized he had a problem. The door to his cabin had been busted open and it hadn't been fixed. Anybody could be in there with a gun aimed at the door waiting for him. He stopped and tried to figure out what to do. The second he stepped through the door he could be a dead man.

So. Was he going to spend the rest of the night outside, hiding in the dark?

No. He'd go in.

He had the Colt in his right hand and the hammer back. Breathing with shallow breaths, he stood to the right of the door, reached out with his left hand and pushed the door open a few inches. It creaked on its iron hinges. That was the only sound. He pushed it farther. Still no sound.

Now what?

All right, the thing to do was to get inside fast and get up against the wall next to the door. Get through the door as fast as he could. All right. He gripped the Colt, took a deep breath and jumped through the door. Immediately, he sidestepped out of the doorway and backed against the wall. No guns boomed. Nothing happened.

He waited and listened until he was sure he was alone in the room, then holstered the Colt and reached for a match. He had no more matches. Couldn't even light the lamp. Oh well, he wasn't sure he wanted to light the lamp anyway. That would be a signal to anybody who might be watching that he was back.

He was tired of poking around in the dark, but he had no choice. Working by feel, he shut the door, found the bed and pushed it up against the door. Next, he found his bedroll on the floor, unrolled it, pulled off his boots and crawled between the blankets.

Sleep wouldn't come. He closed his eyes and tried, but he kept remembering that dream he'd had, the one with Baylor and the rattlesnake. Couldn't get it out of his mind. And suddenly his eyes were wide open and his heart was beating

149

like a tom-tom.

Did something move at the foot of his bed? Yeah. There was something in the bed with him, something that moved slowly. Very slowly. The word popped into his mind:

RATTLESNAKE.

With a loud "Whuh," he jerked his feet out of the bed, threw back the blanket and tarp and bounded up. The dry buzzing of a rattlesnake came from the foot of the bed.

God damn.

He couldn't see it in the dark, but he could damn well hear it. The dry rattle had an angry sound. He'd seen a hundred of them, and he knew the snake was coiled with its head reared back, ready to strike.

His pulse was racing, but he dared not move. It stopped buzzing, but that didn't help a bit. Now it was probably crawling. Which way was it crawling? Where was the damned thing? How many steps to the bed? The only safe place in the room was on the bed. A snake couldn't get up there. But could he make it to the bed without being bitten?

Hell, it was either try or stand here perfectly still until daylight. And daylight was still four or five hours away. He pictured in his mind the location of the bed. He could get there in two long steps. Long fast steps. All he could do was hope the snake wasn't between him and the bed and was too far away to reach him. It couldn't reach far. Only about half the distance of its length. A few feet. He listened, wishing he could hear it and tell from the sound where it was.

One way to find out was to move. Only a slight movement was all it would take. The snake would either strike, with its mouth wide open and its fangs seeking flesh, or it would buzz a warning. Which?

How long did it take a man to die from snakebite? Depended on where he was bitten. He'd seen a hundred cows that had been snakebitten. Mostly on the jaws. Their jaws had swelled up, and they were miserable for a time, but they survived. Well, not always. He remembered one cow that was in the lead of a bunch of cattle he was moving. She'd jumped sideways, and he saw a rattlesnake hanging from her throat, its fangs sunk in so deep it couldn't get loose. The cow took a few more steps, then fell over on her side, kicked a couple of times and died.

A man? If a man was bitten in an artery, he'd die within a few minutes.

Got to move. Move fast, but move. Do it. Now.

In two long steps he was at the edge of the bed, barking his shins against the steel frame. He fell across the bed, face-down, raising his feet and legs off the floor. The snake set up an angry buzzing somewhere near the door.

He was safe. Scrambling to a sitting position, he sat with his arms around his knees and listened to the angry, dry rattling. Soon the rattling stopped, and he knew the reptile was moving again, moving across the floor in the dark.

A team of mules couldn't have dragged him off that bed.

Safe for the moment. The snake couldn't climb up on the bed, the bed was shoved against the door, and he had his Colt six-gun. Yeah, he was safe. But for how long? Somebody had put the snake in his bed. Somebody had caught it alive out on the prairie, probably by throwing a heavy tarp over it. That somebody had unrolled his bed, put the snake in it and rolled it up again. It wasn't a prank. Real outdoorsmen didn't play pranks with snakes. Only estupidos did that. Twice now, somebody had tried to kill him.

What would they try next?

Chapter Twenty

He dozed a while, woke up, wondered where the snake was, dozed again. At daylight, he looked around the room, under the bed, around the room again, and finally saw the snake stretched out near the stove. Moving carefully, he reached for his boots and pulled them on, then made his way to the door. The reptile sensed movement, coiled and buzzed its tail. It as a big one, all right. A good five feet long.

Outside, Lawton went to the stables, took the catch rope off his saddle and picked up a rake used to clean stalls. He went back and opened the door to his cabin. The snake was coiled near the bed. Lawton built a small loop in his rope and, with an overhand throw, pitched the loop around the snake. He dragged it writhing and buzzing outside and beat it to death with the rake. Next, he carried it on the end of the rake to the edge of the yard and threw it over the fence into some weeds. That was done.

Shaving out of a bucket of cold water was a ticklish business, and he nicked himself with the straight razor twice. Finished, he looked at himself in the small mirror and shook his head sadly. What a mess. One eye was still colored from the beating he'd taken, a white bandage covered one side of his neck, and he was bleeding from two razor nicks.

"Lawton Coop," he muttered, "you are one sorry-looking

hombre. If a horned toad was as ugly as you are, it'd have a hell of a time finding a mate."

At least he had one more change of clothes. He rummaged through his warbag for the wrinkled but clean clothes he'd brought, and changed from the skin out. He felt better, but he sure could use a bath. Grinning to himself, he allowed, "The only thing worse than putting clean socks on dirty feet is putting clean britches on a dirty ass." When he looked again in the mirror, he was pleased to see that the razor nicks had stopped bleeding. After he washed the blood off he didn't look quite so bad.

"See you're still around." The counterman just had to say something.

"Still around and still alive. And hungry as a pet bear."

"Got some fresh pork this mornin'."

"Just what I need."

He was left alone while he ate, but his meal was not a leisurely one. His mind was working, worrying. There had to be something else he could do, more questions he could ask. What? At least his jaw wasn't sore anymore. The bacon was good and so were the hotcakes.

The sun was up by the time he finished his meal, and he walked. He didn't want to go back to the wagon camp until he had to. That wasn't a pleasant place. He walked up one side of Commerce Street and down the other. Pedestrians stared at him, and when he found himself on a collision course with a man, he was the one who stepped aside. Women shot him a glance and looked quickly away. He could go back to the county clerk's office and look at land transactions again. But what good would that do? And Mrs. Willis had told him everything she knew about Orville Jackson's death, everything he could think of to ask. The banker, Benjamin Mock, had a ready answer for everything.

Walking aimlessly, he ran Benjamin Mock through his

153

mind. Try as he might, he could find no flaw in the man's answers. In fact, he seemed to be a pretty decent sort of feller. A nice feller, somebody had said. Yeah. Real nice.

While he was thinking of Benjamin Mock, he saw him. Saw him approaching from the direction of his house. Walking right along, happy with the world and everything in it. Too far away to speak to. Didn't have anything to say to him anyway. He turned into the bank building.

That gave Lawton an idea.

Naw. It was a dumb idea. Estupido. What could he possibly gain by it? Forget it. But he couldn't forget it. He stopped where the sidewalk ended and sat on the tailgate of an old freight wagon. A wheel had come off the wagon, and somebody had just left it here in the weeds.

All right, he'd broken into one house and gotten away with it. Could he do it again? Naw. He'd broken into the home of the late Sheriff Spates in the dark. If he broke into Benjamin Mock's house he'd have to do it in the daylight. In fact, he'd have to do it now. Before his housekeeper, Mrs. Willis, came along. What could he hope to find? What had he hoped to find in the sheriff's house?

Of all the ideas that had popped into his head, this was the dumbest.

He got to his feet and walked to Benjamin Mock's house.

The piñons and scrub cedars hid the house from the neighbors to the west, but the front door was in plain sight of the nearest house to the east, about a hundred yards east. Glancing around to see if he was being watched, Lawton walked around to the back. The little house, the toilet, was about fifty feet to the rear in the cedars. The back door was visible to the neighbors. He tried to open it, couldn't. He walked around the west side again, and stopped before a window. A low window. He tried to raise it. It was latched from the inside.

154

Well, that was that. He started to go, then noticed that the latch was a simple hook and eye. He could see it through the glass. As an experiment, he opened the longest blade on his pocketknife and tried to slide it under the wood window frame. He had to do some pushing and twisting, but he could see the blade come into contact with the hook. Barely. The blade wasn't quite long enough to make solid contact.

After another look around, he used the blade to whittle off a piece of the window frame. About half an inch. Then he pushed the blade under the frame again, right where he'd whittled. This time it reached the hook, and he was able to push the hook out of the eye.

Now he folded the knife, put it in his pocket and took another long look around. The window went up easily. It was low enough that he didn't have to climb in head first. He stepped through, pushing aside the lace curtains. It was a bedroom with the bed unmade. Benjamin Mock left bed-making to his hired woman.

Where to look? And what to look for?

He walked through the house, trying to walk quietly, then realized that wasn't necessary. A big main room, a kitchen, a bedroom and another room with a locked door.

Uh-oh. Nobody locked a door without a reason. This was the room to search. But how to get in? He could ram the door with his shoulder and bust it open. No, he'd rather nobody knew he'd been in the house. Squatting, he peered through the keyhole. He could see a desk, but his range of vision was too limited to see anything else. Somehow, he had to get into that room. That's what he'd come here for.

He tried the knife blade, pushed it into the keyhole, pushed it between the lock and the door jamb. It didn't work.

The room had to have a window. Maybe he could open the window of that room from the outside. Naw, the room was on the east side of the house. The neighbors would see him.

Lawton was standing there, trying to figure a way to get into the room when he heard a key in the lock at the

155

front door.

Desperate, he looked for a way out. To get to the back door he'd have to go through the kitchen. He'd never make it without being seen. He could run and hope he wouldn't be recognized. He would be, though.

He had to do something.

Moving with long quick steps he crossed the main room and ducked into the bedroom. In there he could hide. Under the bed if necessary. He got into the room and around the door just as the front door opened and someone came in. Whoever it was walked with heavy steps. Not Mrs. Willis. Had to be Benjamin Mock. Hope the sonofabitch didn't come back to change clothes.

Lawton moved quietly and slipped behind the bedroom door. He tried not to breathe. Footsteps crossed the main room, went into the kitchen. Someone pumped water, only a cup full, and took a drink. The footsteps came back into the main room, stopped, went to the locked door. A key was inserted with a metallic click into the lock. The door was opened.

Maybe he could sneak out now. Naw. He'd be heard. What would he do if the man came into the bedroom? There was a tall wardrobe against the far wall with a hinged door. Could he hide in there? Naw. If the man came into the bedroom to change clothes, he'd open the wardrobe. Under the bed. That's the only place.

But damn, he'd hate to be caught hiding under a bed. He'd be laughed out of town. He'd never live it down. Even if he went home and left Trinidad far behind, he'd always remember the humiliation. No, by God, he'd stay put. If he was found, he'd be found standing up like a man.

Footsteps again. They came out of the locked room, crossed the main room, went into the kitchen and out the back door. To the toilet? Yeah, whoever he was, he had to heed the call of nature. Now was the time to get the hell out of here.

Lawton tip-toed into the main room, heading for the front door. Surely, the front door was unlocked now. As he passed the room on the east side, he saw it was wide open. The man, Benjamin Mock, or whoever he was, had left it open, planning to be back in a few minutes.

A few minutes? Couldn't take much of a look in a few minutes, but hell . . .

With a glance at the kitchen, Lawton stepped inside the room. There was a desk, a cabinet and a narrow cot. The desk would be the best bet. Moving quickly, he opened the top drawer, rummaged through papers. Bank papers, mostly. The Merchants Bank of Las Animas County. Here was a deed to some land. More legal descriptions. Bank documents.

Hurry, damnit, and find something.

His fingers felt thick and clumsy as he ruffled through more papers. More bank business. Here was an envelope from the First National Bank of Pueblo. He fumbled it open, took out a letter and started reading, hastily. The letter was written in ink in a beautiful hand.

"Mr. Benjamin L. Mock,
"Dear Sir,
"In reference to account number 194 . . ."

Uh-oh. He heard the door slam on the toilet. He had to leave. Now.

Quickly, he shut the desk drawer and headed for the front door. He yanked it open and stepped through. He closed the door behind him just as the kitchen door was opened.

Instead of running for the road, he ran south into the cedars, and kept running until he came to a shallow draw. There he stopped, lay on his belly and watched the house behind him. Where he was on the edge of a draw he could be hard to see from the house, but he could see the front door clearly. He watched.

157

Within a few minutes a man came out, a well-dressed man. Benjamin Mock. He was in no hurry, didn't glance around as if he was looking for a thief. He locked the door behind him and strolled away toward the bank. Lawton watched him until he was out of sight, then stood. It would seem, he thought, that Benjamin Mock hadn't discovered yet that his desk had been rifled. It would seem that he'd come back from the toilet, locked everything up and gone to his office. But he would notice, sooner or later, that somebody had been in his desk. And he would see where the window had been forced open. He would wonder who, and he just might suspect Lawton. Who else? A thief? It could have been a thief looking for something valuable to steal. More than likely, though, it was someone looking into Benjamin Mock's personal affairs. And that someone had to be Lawton Coop.

Nothing was stolen, but even so it was illegal to break into another man's house. The banker would have the sheriff asking questions of Lawton. The sheriff probably wouldn't have enough evidence to arrest him, but he would keep a suspicious eye on him. Benjamin Mock too would answer no more questions from him. The whole thing would make his mission more difficult.

And worse, he hadn't learned a damned thing. It was all for nothing.

He didn't want to be seen coming from the direction of the banker's house, so he took a roundabout route to the wagon camp. There, the boy, Thomas Watkins, was at work raking stalls. He saw Lawton coming.

"Mr. Coop, I see they didn't fix your door yet." The boy was bareheaded, and a sheaf of sun-bleached hair hung across his forehead.

"Naw. If I had a hammer and a saw and some nails I'd fix it myself. Are you gonna be working here for a few more days?"

"Yeah. Until Pa gits better. His shoulder still hurts and he can't hardly move it. I'm workin' for our board here."

"Would you do me a favor and keep an eye on my cabin? I've got things to do and I can't stay here and watch it."

"Sure. I've been doin' that most of the time anyway."

"Did you see anybody go into it last night?"

"Naw, but I wasn't watchin' after dark. Why? Was somethin' stole?"

"No, but all kinds of people stay in a place like this. You have to keep your eyes open."

"I surely will, you betcha."

Inside the cabin, he sat on the bed with his head in his hands and was depressed. The whole trip had been for nothing. He'd accomplished nothing. Breaking into the late sheriff's house was dumb. Breaking into Benjamin Mock's house was dumb. What had he found? Personal letters in the late sheriff's house. Bank papers in the banker's house. Nothing out of the ordinary. Nothing that he couldn't have expected to find. Nothing he'd hoped to find. Just papers.

Wait a minute.

His head came up and puzzled thoughts went through his mind. Bank papers? The late sheriff had an envelope from the First National Bank of Pueblo, and so did Benjamin Mock. The letter that came in the sheriff's envelope was missing, but the letter that came in Benjamin Mock's envelope .... Damn, he wished he'd had time to read that letter. Could he go back and read it? Nope. Impossible. What did it say, the little that he did get to read?

Dear Mr. Mock, it said. In reference to account number ... what? One-ninety-four? Yeah, that's what it was, 194. It had to mean something.

He stood and walked across the room, head down. Walked back and sat on the bed again. It meant something, all right. It meant Benjamin Mock had an account in the First National Bank of Pueblo. The sheriff had had an account there too. Now, why would the president of a bank in Trinidad have an account in a bank in Pueblo? Didn't he trust his own bank? His bank was robbed once, and it was

159

easy. Was he afraid of being robbed again and didn't want to keep his own money in it? Hell of a way for a banker to think. Hell of a note when the sheriff doesn't trust the bank either.

Oh. For the second time that morning a brilliant idea popped into his mind. He turned it over and studied it. Yeah. It meant something, that was a fact. He had a notion what, but he wasn't sure. He intended to find out.

Chapter Twenty-One

The wagon camp owner came to the door in his undershirt, belly hanging over the waist of his pants, hair uncombed, needing a shave. "Yeah?"

"Do you know—can you tell me when the stage leaves for Pueblo?"

He belched and picked at his teeth with a fingernail. "I b'leve they change horses at Uncle Dick's toll house, and git down here about ten-thirty."

"Do you know when they get to Pueblo?"

"Sometime in the night, I b'leve."

"Much obliged." He hunted up the boy, Thomas Watkins, found him pushing a wheelbarrow full of manure. "There's a dollar in it for you if you see that my two horses are fed and watered for a couple of days. Make that three days."

"Sure, you betcha."

"You'll do that for me now, won't you?"

"You betcha, Mr. Coop. I surely will."

That arranged, he headed for the hotel where he'd seen the stage load and unload passengers. He walked as fast as he could without running. He hoped he wasn't too late.

Horses' backs were a hell of a lot more comfortable than

the inside of a Concord coach. Lawton estimated he had fifteen inches of seat, with a fat man on one side of him and a woman with a baby on the other side. Two men and a woman with two children faced him on the opposite seat. There was barely room for all their feet, and their feet often got tangled up. To make matters worse, Lawton was riding backwards. Every time the coach hit a bump, the passengers bounced so high their heads touched the roof. Everyone noticed the bandage on Lawton's neck, but no one said anything. The fat man started sweating fifteen minutes out of Trinidad. He smelled like a wet dog. Then the youngest child across from him began crying. The child's mother was apologetic.

"We've come all the way from Santa Fe, and we're going to stay with my folks in Denver. Lord, I wish we were there."

Lawton offered to hold her other youngster, and the woman gladly handed her over. She was about three years old and afraid of Lawton. He didn't know what to do, and he wished he hadn't offered to hold her.

"He's a nice man, Eloise," the woman cooed. "He won't hurt you." The younger one, less than a year old, cried, and Lawton wondered how anything so small could be so loud.

By the time they left the first relay station, the three-year-old had decided that Lawton was no one to fear, and she wanted to tell him about her dog at home and her daddy. "My dog's name is Patches, and my daddy went on a long journey." Lawton was afraid to ask what that meant. He looked quizzically at the woman. The woman shook her head sadly.

"Well, uh, how old is your dog?" He didn't know what else to say.

"I dunno. He's 'bout as old as I am. What happened to your neck?"

"Oh, nothing much. Just got cut a little."

"Oh."

It occurred to Lawton that this was something he had to

get used to. He was soon to become a father, and he would soon be holding his own kid on his lap, talking to him. Or her. He had to learn to talk to children. But he'd be darned if he knew what to say.

In the late afternoon, the teamster "Whoaed" the four-up and the coach came to a stop. He hollered down, "Got to wait for the southbound, folks. Got to wait here whar it's easy to pass. Won't be long. I saw 'er comin' when we went over that last rise." Sure enough, in a few minutes another Concord, also pulled by four horses, rattled past. Someone yelled, "Hiya, Bert." Passengers leaned out the windows and waved to passengers going the opposite direction. Then, "Git up, thar. You, Queenie, hit that collar. Git up, Prince. Git in thar." The Concord lurched forward.

An hour later it dipped into a sandy draw and was stuck. Four horses lunged into their collars, but couldn't pull it out of the deep sand. Passengers had to get out and push. With everyone pushing and the horses pulling, the wheels came out of the sand and rolled out of the draw.

"Lucky we didn't bust an axle," the teamster allowed. "All right, ever'body git aboard. The next stop is four or five mile." He pulled a biscuit-sized stemwinder watch out of a shirt pocket. "We're still on the money."

At the next relay station, the passengers got out, went to the toilet and stretched their legs. A long bench inside the adobe building held four wash basins where passengers could wash their faces. There was soap and an endless towel on a roller. One mirror hung on a wall, and a comb, hairbrush, and even a toothbrush hung from long strings. Passengers could use them, but not carry them away. No one used the toothbrush. Fresh horses were hitched to the Concord, and the teamster bawled, "All 'board. We're fixin' to git goin'."

That was why Lawton was riding the stage instead of his dun horse. By changing horses three times, the teamster was able to keep them at a high trot nearly all the way, and somewhere around ten o'clock that night, the stage arrived with a rattle of trace chains and singletrees in front of the Arkansas Hotel in Pueblo.

The fat man's big tin suitcase was handed down to him from the top of the coach. He wiped his face with a blue bandana and said he was looking forward to a good meal, a bath and a soft bed. The woman with the two kids climbed out stiffly with Lawton's help, and allowed she would get only a short rest before boarding the stage to Colorado City. From Colorado City, she would start the long journey to Denver. "Lord, I wish we was there," she said.

It was a two-story, clapboard hotel with a few chairs scattered across a small lobby. Lawton rented a room on the second floor and made arrangements for a bath in the hotel's water closet on the first floor. When he signed the register, he was told that he had taken the last room available. Before visiting the water closet, he headed for the hotel's dining room and some supper, and when he came out he saw the woman and her two youngsters sprawled in wooden chairs in the lobby. He approached.

"Pardon me, ma'am, but I understand the stage won't leave for a couple of hours. I've rented a room upstairs and I haven't touched the bed. Why don't you and the kids go up there and rest until the stage leaves? I'll be sure to wake you up when it's time."

She looked at him with weary eyes. "Where will you sleep, mister?"

"I'll stay up. I'd kind of like to take a look around town anyway. I've never been in Pueblo before."

"I sure do thank you, mister." She stood, picked up the baby and tried to awaken the little girl. "I'll carry her," Lawton said.

Inside the room, he put the child carefully on the bed and turned to go.

"The Lord'll bless you, mister. He surely will."

Outside, he took two deep breaths of the cool night air,

nd mumbled to himself. "Oh well, two nights without sleep won't kill me. Make that one-and-a-half nights."

Pueblo was a bigger town than Trinidad, older, with a treet full of businesses of all kinds. The Arkansas River oured off the Continental Divide to the west, passed in ront of the town and went on its way east. There were a few amps hanging outside the storefronts, and most of the vindows were lighted. Only a few horsebackers and edestrians were on the street. Lawton walked on planks for wo blocks, crossed the street and walked back. The First National Bank of Pueblo was in the next block, another rick building with a split shingle roof. The windows and the loor were protected by steel bars. Lamps burning inside vould illuminate any hoodlum who managed to break in, nd if the lamps were extinguished, the night marshal would e immediately suspicious.

Lawton looked in the store windows, at new saddles in a addle and harness shop, at new clothes in a clothing mporium, at shovels, picks and crowbars in a hardware tore. Finally, he went back to the hotel and sat in the lobby. And sat.

No saddle ever was as hard as that chair. His discomfort eminded him of a hired hand they'd had for a while on the Circle C. The man was always moaning, "Oh, my achin' ead, ass and back." Other men on the ranch got to referring o him as "Old Achin' Ass."

He was dozing fitfully when the Concord and four-up topped in front of the hotel. He could see by the lamplight hat the horses were all bays. Good stout horses of around welve hundred and fifty pounds. A handsome team. A boy f about eighteen held the lead horses by their bridles while he teamster climbed down from his high seat and came into he lobby. "Whar's the lady and young'uns?"

"I'll get them," Lawton said, standing and straightening is knees slowly. He had to knock on the door three times efore he got a response. The woman opened the door, sleep in her eyes. Without a word she gathered her children, carried the youngest and led the three-year-old by the hand down the stairs.

The teamster spoke to her through his tobacco-stained beard, "You got time to go to the, uh, uh, if you want to. I'll wait fer yuh, but I cain't wait long.

"Leastways," he said to Lawton after the woman and her kids had headed for the ladies' water closet, "it won't be crowded in thar tonight. Only two other passengers. She can lay the young'uns down on the seat."

After the stage rattled away, Lawton decided on a bath first and then the bed. At that time of night he had the water closet to himself, though the water that came out of the wood-burning water heater was only lukewarm. The fire had died out. Bed, when he finally crawled into it, was paradise. It made him feel like he was floating. His only worry was he'd oversleep. The bank opened at nine o'clock, he'd been told, and the southbound stage pulled out around ten.

But he worried for nothing. A cattleman, used to getting out of bed at daylight, couldn't have overslept if he'd wanted to.

He had breakfast in the hotel's dining room, seated at a table all to himself. That over, he went to his room, looked at himself in a mirror and wished he'd brought a razor so he could shave. Then after thinking it over a few seconds, he decided he didn't want to shave. He combed his hair with his fingers and went out on the street.

Pueblo was alive. All kinds of traffic passed the hotel—heavy freight wagons loaded with trade goods, gold prospectors leading burros carrying a bed and groceries, pack mules bearing furs down from the mountains, buggies driven by well-dressed men, cowboys riding at a slow trot. Lawton stood on the plank walk across the street from the First National Bank of Pueblo and waited for it to open.

And while he waited, he wondered whether he'd be able to do what he had in mind to do. Just thinking about it caused

166

his stomach to churn and a lump to form in his throat. Could he fool everybody? Was he a good enough actor? Was Benjamin Mock known by sight in the bank? Did he make a trip for nothing? He was nervous and impatient at the same time.

Come on, he muttered under his breath, open the damn bank. Let's get this over with.

Chapter Twenty-Two

At straight up nine o'clock a middle-aged man in a long coat, a vest and gray-striped trousers opened the front door. His thick brown hair was parted in the middle, and he had a thick moustache. Lawton crossed the street and was right behind him when he finished unlocking the door and reentered the bank lobby. Just inside, Lawton paused. The lobby was as ornate as anything he'd seen in Santa Fe or anywhere else. A marble floor, two waist-high tables for writing, wrought-iron tellers' cages and a wrought-iron knee-high fence between the lobby and the executive offices. There were four tellers. Which would be the least suspicious? The youngest-looking or the oldest? The youngest would be unsure of himself and would get permission from someone older before he did anything unusual. The older man had probably seen and heard everything, and he'd be hard to fool. All right, the middle-aged one.

"Yes sir." The teller looked up. He was balding, and his moustache was so thin it looked as if it had been painted on. He wore a striped shirt with no collar, buttoned tightly at the throat.

Lawton's mind was working. Now is the time to act like a man of means, a man who knows what he's doing, who has done this many times. He cleared his throat, and said in his

168

best voice, "Please excuse my appearance. I've been inspecting some mining claims, and I'm on my way back to Trinidad. I want to look at the deposit and withdrawal records of my account number one hundred and ninety-four."

"Yes sir. One ninety-four?"

"Yes. That's my personal account."

"Well, sir." The teller was hesitant. "Would you give me your name, sir?"

"Mock. Benjamin Mock."

"A moment, please, sir." The teller turned and went into an executive office near a shiny steel safe that was as big as a barn door.

Uh-oh, Lawton thought. He's suspicious. His stomach began churning faster and his hands began to tremble. It wasn't going to work. This was foolish. He'd come to Pueblo for nothing. In fact, he'd be lucky if he didn't get in trouble with the law. He waited. Come on, damnit, do something. Let's get this over with.

Other customers came into the lobby and approached the other tellers.

Finally, the executive office opened and the teller came out accompanied by the well-dressed gentleman who had unlocked the front door. The man was smiling a polite smile. Lawton put a small frown on his face, what he hoped was an impatient frown.

"Mr. Mock." The well-dressed gent approached the teller's cage and held out his hand to shake. "Nice to see you again." His eyes went over Lawton from the riding boots to the wide-brim hat, stopped for a second on the bandaged neck.

"Nice to see you again, too, sir." Lawton shook with him. "As I told this young man, I've been inspecting some mining claims west of here and I'm on my way back to Trinidad. Due to some other financial transactions, I've become slightly, uh, shall we say confused, over my balance here."

169

"I see. Do you wish to make a withdrawal?"

"No sir. I only wish to look at the record of transactions and the balance."

"Yes sir." The banker's eyes narrowed for a second, and he made no immediate move. Lawton could guess what was going on in his mind: This man here in rancher's clothes could be Benjamin Mock. He is approximately the right size with the right kind of face. Dressed as he is and unshaved he would look a little different. At least, that's what Lawton hoped he was thinking. He also hoped he was thinking: Well, he isn't asking for a withdrawal, just to inspect his banking statement.

"Very well, Mr. Mock. Robert, will you show Mr. Mock his transaction record?"

"Yes sir," the teller said. "How far back do you wish to go, Mr. Mock?"

"Only for the past year."

"Yes sir." He turned and headed toward another door.

"Have a good day, Mr. Mock." The banker held out his hand to shake again. Lawton shook with him. "Thank you, sir."

He could feel sweat under his armpits and he hoped it didn't show on his face. How long was that teller going to be gone? How damn long did it take? Come on, damnit, let's get this over with.

"Here you are, Mr. Mock." The teller was back. He handed Lawton a sheet of paper. "Would you care to study this in privacy, sir?"

"No, I think I can see all I need to see in a few seconds." There wasn't much to see. Everything was in black ink, written in a beautiful hand. No figures at all in the withdrawal column. The deposit column had four figures. The first three were small amounts, none over six hundred dollars. But the last figure caused Lawton's pulse to quicken. Eighteen thousand dollars. All at one time. And the deposit was made on October 6, 1869. He glanced at the teller to see

170

if the teller was watching him. He was. He tried to keep his face straight and his voice normal.

"Hmm," he muttered, as if absorbing the figures. "I see. Hmm. Well, thank you very much." He handed the sheet back to the teller.

"Whew," he said under his breath when he stepped outside onto the planks. "Glad that's over. Now to get the hell out of town."

At the hotel, he was told again that the southbound stage came through at ten o'clock. Sometimes it arrived early, but it never left early. He went to his room and splashed water on his face.

Looking at himself in the mirror again, he tried a small smile. "Lawton Coop, you sonofagun, if you could read Shakespeare you could get a job trodding the boards. Or whatever the hell those actors call it."

With time to kill he walked toward the river, following a dirt path between the buildings and across weed-grown vacant lots. More Mexican children playing in the streets, ragged, barefoot. At the river, he threw a rock out to the middle of it, watched it splash and sink, then turned and walked back, taking another route a block west. He found himself on a street of saloons and houses with red lanterns hanging from the front doors. The lanterns were not lighted. Another block, and he saw the stage company's relay station. Four horses were harnessed and tied to a hitchrack, waiting their turn at the southbound. He walked on. Back at the hotel, he started to enter the lobby, paused.

What if that banker got suspicious and reported him to the town marshal or the county sheriff? Best stay out of the hotel until the stage left. He crossed the street and stood with his back against a board building and watched the hotel entrance.

Aw hell, he said under his breath, this wasn't necessary. If anyone was suspicious he'd have had the law on him before he got out of the bank. Besides, he didn't take any money or

171

anything. Hell, he hadn't done anything illegal. Go wait in the lobby. No, he'd spend enough time sitting when he got on the stage. Better stand while he had a chance.

In about thirty minutes the stage pulled up in front of the hotel. The horses were fresh, stamping their feet and slobbering on the bridle bits. Lawton bought his ticket and got aboard. There were not as many passengers going south as there had been going north, and he had to share a seat with only two men. But he had to sit on the wrong side again and ride backwards. Three men sat on the opposite side. Lawton not only had to ride backwards, he had to sit in the middle. The other passengers had gotten on board first, and they weren't about to give up their window seats.

Traveling south from Pueblo, he saw the Colorado that he hadn't seen in the dark the night before. The terrain was varied—from rocky hills covered with piñon to desert as flat as a fritter. A few miles west, where the mountains rose out of the foothills, the country was entirely different. Steep. That was something they didn't have in the Pecos Valley.

With so little sleep in the past forty-eight hours, Lawton found himself fighting to stay awake. Then he decided it would do no harm to doze off, and he scooted down in his seat, tilted his hat over his eyes and let sleep take over.

At the first relay station, he got out and walked a way to get the kinks out of his legs and to give his backside a rest. He was barely able to suppress a groan when he got back in and sat on the thinly padded seat again. He had hoped that one of the passengers would stay at the relay station so he could have a window seat, but no such luck. A passenger across from him had started the day well dressed, but now he loosened the cravat at his throat, pushed back his derby hat and wiped his red face with a large white handkerchief. His face was covered with dust kicked up by the horses' hooves and blown back inside the coach. Seeing that made Lawton glad he was riding backwards.

172

"Do you have to make this trip very much?" he asked Lawton.

"Naw. This was my first trip to Pueblo."

"I have to do this ever' few months. Sellin' hardware. It's a hell of a way to make a livin'."

"Yeah," Lawton said, not feeling much like a conversation. "This could get old in a hurry."

"I got to find another job. At least till the railroad gets here."

"They say it's coming."

"Yeh," another passenger put in. "It's already got to Cheyenne, and it's headin' south. That's what the Denver papers said. They said another railroad is comin' from the east, and in a couple years there'll be two railroads in Denver."

"I've heard the one heading south will come all the way to Trinidad. Another one is coming from the east somewhere and they'll meet at Trinidad."

"That's what the paper said. It's a race to see which one gets there first."

Lawton scooted down in his seat and tilted his hat over his eyes again. "It's gonna be interesting."

At the next relay station he bought a plate of beans and bread, and had just wolfed it down when the stage from the south pulled up. Eight passengers got out, stiffly, sorely. Six men and two women. Two of the men offered helping hands to the women when they stepped out, but another, a man in business clothes, ignored the women, slapped the dust off his sleeves, and headed toward the toilets, determined to be the first there.

Lawton swallowed the last bite of bread, stood, and his mouth dropped open.

Benjamin Mock.

When the banker saw Lawton he stopped suddenly. The two men stared at each other a moment, and finally Lawton

173

nodded and said, "How do, Mr. Mock."

Benjamin Mock said nothing, only stared.

And Lawton knew, as a tired team of horses was led awa
and a fresh team was brought up and hitched to th
singletrees, that the chance meeting with the banker mean
trouble.

From here on, he said under his breath, I'm gonna have t
work fast.

Chapter Twenty-Three

It was a bone-weary Lawton Coop who climbed sorely out of the Concord in front of the Trinidad Hotel that night. He didn't know what time it was, but it had been dark for over two hours. The horses with their good night vision had followed the wagon road into town. But, though the horses could find their way over the Raton Pass, they couldn't be trusted to keep the coach wheels from falling off the edge of the road. The coach would go no farther until daylight. Trinidad was dark and quiet—except for loud haw-haws coming from El Raton down the street. He walked in the dark to the wagon yard, found his rented cabin, noticed that the door hadn't been fixed, and stepped inside.

Light from a sulphur match showed him his pack panniers and bed were still there. He lit the lamp, worried that he made a good target in the lamplight, but knowing he wasn't about to crawl into his bed without looking it over. Again, he shoved the spring bed up against the door, then shook out the blankets and tarp of his own bed. Satisfied that nothing dangerous was in the room, he pulled off his boots, blew out the lamp and got between the blankets.

As tired as he was, he couldn't sleep right away. His heart was heavy when he thought of Mary and wondered whether he'd make it back home before the baby came. He had a powerful urge to get right back to work on his chore here in Trinidad. Now. Not after daylight. No time to spare. But he had no choice. He had to wait for morning.

At the crack of dawn he was up. He dressed, saw that his horses were well fed and cared for, and went to breakfast. For his stomach's sake, he forced himself to chew slowly. The counterman stood in front of him and just had to say something.

"When I didn't see you yesterday, I figgered you went back south or was dead. See I was wrong on both counts."

Speaking around a mouthful of sausage, Lawton said, "You're gonna be right on one count or the other pretty damned soon." He washed the sausage and hotcakes down with a cup of black coffee. It all sat heavily on his stomach, but he couldn't blame the food. It was that terrible feeling of urgency.

Things were going to start popping in Trinidad in the next couple of days. He could feel it. But he had some things to do first, more questions to ask. Slow down, he reminded himself. Don't make any mistakes.

Dr. Hiram Bromley was in, but he had a patient. Lawton had to wait outside. He waited. He sat on the ground under a cedar and waited. The patient was a woman, he'd seen that much when the doctor had opened the door for a second. Waited. Finally, she came out, straightening her long dress and buttoning the bodice. He got a glimpse of white bandage on her chest. She was Mexican, young and pretty. No wonder the doctor took so long. When the door opened again and he was beckoned inside, he could see that the doctor's hair was wet, and he guessed he'd just washed his face and combed his hair.

It was none of his business.

"You are Mr., uh, Coop, aren't you?"

"Yeah, Doctor. I think this bandage can come off now,

but I'd like for you to look at it to be sure. Don't want to get infected."

Nodding at a chair, Dr. Bromley said, "Sit down there and let's have a look." Lawton sat. The doctor took hold of one end of the bandage and murmured, "This will sting a little," and he ripped the bandage off. Lawton winced, but kept his mouth shut.

"Hmm. I think we'd better put a fresh patch on this. It would be foolish to take unnecessary chances."

"All right. Uh, doctor, can I ask you something?"

"About what?"

"Poison. Mercury. Have you had any experience with it?"

"Umm. No, can't say that I have. Why do you ask?"

"Oh, no particular reason. Do you, uh, does any of your doctor books have anything to say about it?"

"Well now, let's see." Doctor Bromley went to the shelf containing his collection of books, selected one and opened it. "Mmm. Let's see. Mercury, eh? Here it is."

"Can I have a look?"

"Well, this is very unusual, but . . . I suppose so." He handed the book, opened, to Lawton. It was a large handsomely bound book, titled *Doctor Hauser's Book of Poisons*.

Lawton quickly found the heading, "Mercury." As he read, his eyebrows went up. Mercury was also known as quicksilver. ". . . fatalities have occurred from 0.2 gm. Symptoms: profuse vomiting of mucoid material and fluid . . . becomes concentrated in the kidneys . . . causes increase in output of urine . . . bleeding gums . . . death from vascular collapse. Remedy . . ." Closing the book, Lawton handed it back. He had seen enough.

"Why the interest in mercury, Mr. Coop?"

"Oh, uh, it's something these prospectors around here use to separate gold dust from worthless dust. I've heard it can kill a man."

When Hiram Bromley replaced the book, Lawton

177

couldn't help thinking that he probably wasn't a real doctor. A real doctor would know more about poisons, and a real doctor wouldn't have spent so much time bandaging a pretty woman's chest. Hiram Bromley had probably worked in a hospital somewhere, probably as a surgeon's helper, and he knew something about medicine. But sooner or later a real doctor would come to Trinidad and Hiram Bromley would be exposed.

Oh well, Lawton thought, in the meantime he's better than nothing.

With a clean white bandage on the side of his neck, he walked with rapid steps to a small house three blocks away, the small neat house with flowers in the yard. He knocked. And hoped.

The door was opened and immediately slammed shut.

"Please, Mrs. Willis. I need just a little more information from you and then I won't bother you again. That's a promise."

She spoke through the door, "I have answered all your questions, Mr. Coop, and I do not wish to speak with you again."

"Please." He realized he was begging, something he had done very little of in his life. Damn little of. But he was desperate. "Please, Mrs. Willis, I've learned something new and I have to know a little more around Orville Jackson's death. Only one minute, I promise."

"You and your brother are dangerous men. I do not wish to speak to you."

"I am not dangerous. I wouldn't harm a hair on your head." He wished he'd brought Annie Gordon with him, but he hadn't wanted to bother her. "I'll stay outside where the whole world can see me. I'll keep my distance from you. If anything happens you can scream, and my life wouldn't be worth a plugged nickel. Just come outside."

"If you've got a question, ask me through the door."

"All right. Tell me, did Orville Jackson, the night he died,

178

have any, uh, blood around his mouth?"

"Of course. He often coughed up blood."

"I mean, more than usual?"

"He had blood around his mouth. His mouth was open."

"You said you heard him coughing after Sheriff Spates left that night. Did he, uh, was he . . . did he cough the way he always did? I mean, was there anything different about the way he sounded?"

"You're asking a lot of questions, young man. What are you trying to do?"

"Please, can you tell me?"

The door opened a crack, and he could see her face. "Now that I think about it, I'm . . . I'm not sure."

"What do you mean, Mrs. Willis? It's important."

"Why is it so important?"

"I, uh, can't tell you because I'm not sure myself right now. I think I know what happened, but I'm not sure yet. If you'll answer my questions, I'll know then."

She pondered that. "Well, now that I think about it, I seem to recollect he . . . I believe he sounded like he was choking, or gasping, as much as coughing."

"Was there a drinking glass or water pitcher near his bed?"

"Yes. I always kept some fresh water there."

"Was there anything in the glass?"

"I . . . I don't recollect. There could have been."

"One more question, Mrs. Willis, and I won't bother you again. I don't know how to ask, but . . ." He shifted his weight from one foot to the other. "Well, Mrs. Willis, we're both grown people and we know there are things we don't talk much about. Uh, did Mr. Jackson . . . during the night, did he, uh, wet the bed?"

"What? What kind of question is that?"

"It's important. Believe me."

"Not that it's any of your business, but yes, he did."

"Was that unusual? I mean, did he ever do that before?"

"No. He never did."

179

A sigh of relief came from Lawton's lips, and he felt his shoulders and chest relax. "Thank you, Mrs. Willis. You've been a big help. Maybe I . . . maybe I can return the favor." He turned to go, stepped off the porch. "Thanks again."

The Gordons were busy setting type when he came through the open door of the Las Animas Gazette. Annie Gordon dropped what she was doing and hurried to him.

"My gosh, Lawton, where have you been? I've been worried."

Her father came over too, peering over his glasses. "I'm glad to see you. You'd think you were a long lost brother, the way Annie has been acting. She even went to the wagon yard, and when she saw your horses and belongings there she was convinced that your body was lying in a ravine somewhere."

"Well, Lordy, Annie." Lawton felt sheepish, and he couldn't meet her gaze. "I, uh, I went to Pueblo. I decided all of a sudden to go and I didn't have time to tell anybody."

"She even asked the sheriff to look for you."

"I'm sorry, Annie. I really am." Apologizing was something else he wasn't used to, but there were times . . .

"Sit down," she snapped. She was irritated, probably because of the worry he'd caused. Her face was hard and her brown eyes were narrow. "Have some coffee." She spun and went to the stove in the back of the room. When she returned with a coffee cup, he took it, took a sip, and put it on the desk.

He said, "I think you two had better sit down. I've got a story for you."

"What happened?" She was staring intently at him, her face still hard.

"First," Lawton said, "can you tell me one thing? The story I read in your newspaper about the bank robbery and all didn't say how much money was stolen from the bank.

180

Do you happen to know?"

She answered immediately, "Nineteen thousand dollars. It took a few days for the bookkeepers to total it up. It was every dollar the bank had. Now, what's the story?"

Lawton sighed. "It's a long story, but I think I know what went wrong. I mean, what and why. I have to tell somebody, and I'd like to tell you two."

"We're all ears." She was still snapping.

"Are you mad at me, Annie?"

Slowly, her face softened, and her brown eyes were round again. The dimple in her chin wasn't quite so deep. "Well, I was worried. I had no right to be." Then her eyes widened. "Do you mean to say you know what happened to Baylor?"

"Yeah. I know. But I wonder if maybe the sheriff ought to be here. I'd like for him to hear this too."

"I'll go get him." She whirled and was gone.

"This," said James C. Gordon, perching on the stool beside his desk, "sounds like a banner story."

Picking up the coffee cup, Lawton took another sip. "It is, Mr. Gordon. I don't know anything about journalism, and maybe you won't want to print it, but it's a hell of a story."

Gordon shrugged. "We do hear a lot of things we can't print. We can't just run off at the press without proof."

Shaking his head sadly, Lawton said, "It's something the people ought to know. They have a right to know about it."

"Then, by gosh, we'll tell them. One way or another, we'll tell them."

It occurred to Lawton right then that the Gordons, though they had come from the east, were people of conviction and courage. If it came to a fight, they would fight.

With a half-smile, he shook his head again. "Annie once said she's on Baylor's side. Right now you two could be the best friends the Coop brothers ever had."

They were silent as they waited. Lawton finished his coffee. Gordon sat perched on the stool. Lawton remained standing.

When Annie returned she was half-running and pulling Sheriff Horace Willard by a shirtsleeve. Pedestrians on the street were staring open-mouthed.

"Whoa, now, Miss Gordon," Willard said. "What's the gosh-darned hurry?"

"Come on. Hurry, will you."

Inside, she led the sheriff up to Lawton, and gasped, "All right, we're here. Now, talk to us."

Chapter Twenty-Four

Lawton Coop grinned at her urgency, and began, "Well, I believe the best way is to start at . . ."

He was interrupted by James C. Gordon. "I apologize for the shortage of chairs. Please, everyone, make yourselves as comfortable as you can. Mr. Willard, why don't you take the chair, and Mr. Coop, you can sit here on the stool. Annie and I will stand."

The sheriff sat, and pulled at one end of his handlebar moustache. He frowned at Lawton. "Miss Gordon tells me you know things the rest of us don't know. What is it?"

Lawton leaned his buttocks against the desk, facing the sheriff. Annie Gordon sat on the stool. James C. Gordon stood.

"I'll start at the beginning," Lawton said. "I think it's the best way." He paused. Everyone was listening. Choosing his words carefully, and speaking slowly, he went on:

"My brother, Baylor Coop, left home a year ago and went up to the gold camps around Pikes Peak. He didn't find any gold, and he headed back south. For a while, probably a short while, he stopped in Pueblo where he wrote a letter to our mother. That was the last word we got from him. While he was in Pueblo, he heard about some public land west of Trinidad that sounded like good cow country. He came here to claim some of it. He believed, like a lot of folks, that it was public domain and belonged to whoever settled on it first. He even built himself a cabin and a corral. He was planning to bring some cattle up from home and go into the cow business. But then . . ."

Lawton paused to clear his throat. He wasn't used to talking so much. "Then he found out the land wasn't public domain, but belonged to the Maxwell Land Company. As I understand it, that came as quite a surprise to a lot of folks when the U.S. Government ruled that all one million, five hundred thousand acres of the old Maxwell Land Grant really did belong to the Maxwells. A lot of folks still don't believe it. When Mr. Maxwell sold it to some eastern investors, a lot of folks were ordered off their land. What they believed was their land. There was some shooting and some folks killed. But Baylor is a cowman. He's got no use for squatters either. We've had some trouble with squatters at home. Not much, but some. So Baylor knew he had to do one of two things."

Pausing again, Lawton swallowed, shifted positions against the desk. "He could either get off the land or buy it. He didn't have enough money to buy it, but he had a few bucks left, and he got into a poker game. He figured he'd either go broke or he'd buy some land. One or the other. He played with four men in El Raton, and he played wild, figuring he had nothing much to lose. When the dust settled he had all their money. That's when his troubles began."

He had to swallow to moisten his throat. Lawton was a man who could yell at cattle all day without getting hoarse, but talking was something else. Three pairs of eyes were watching him intently. Three pairs of ears were listening.

"When two toughs braced him in El Raton and demanded a chance to win their money back, he told them he didn't have it. He wasn't lying. He'd spent it. What he'd spent it for was land. He, uh, told Annie here he'd bought six hundred acres. And I was told he'd won about a thousand dollars in that poker game. So I'm guessing he paid around a buck-and-a-half an acre. That was two-bits an acre more than he would have paid for government land. But it left him with some money for supplies and building materials and stuff like that.

"Well, the two ranihans didn't believe him, and they called him a liar. Where Baylor and I came from, and around here too, you don't call a man a liar unless you're ready to fight.

"Now, let me tell you something about Baylor. He can fight. He can fight with his fists or with a gun. He doesn't go around looking for fights, and I've even seen him walk away from a feller he didn't want to fight, a feller who was liquored up and didn't know what he was doing, a feller who had a wife and three kids. But he won't take too many insults. Call him a liar and you'd better have a gun in your hand and be ready to use it. Or be seven feet tall.

"So they had a fight. I've been told that the two ranihans drew their six-guns first. Started to, anyway. Baylor is fast with a gun. He just outshot them. That's all there was to that. He had to kill them or get killed. That's the way I heard it and it must be so because he wasn't arrested. In fact, nobody accused him of anything. Not at that time, anyway. It wasn't till later that he ran into trouble with the law. And that was because the law was crooked."

Swallowing, he tried to talk on, but his voice was getting hoarse. He looked toward the pump at the rear of the room, and was thinking about getting himself a drink of water, when Annie suddenly said, "Would you like a drink of water, Lawton? I'll get it."

While he waited, Sheriff Horace Willard put in, "You said the law was crooked. You'd better explain that."

Lawton didn't say any more until the girl returned and he drank a cup of water. "I'll get to that in a minute. What happened next is somebody in the land company decided they'd made a mistake. They shouldn't have sold Baylor that land."

185

Pausing, clearing his throat, he went on: "Have you ever wondered why there is some land just west of town that they won't sell? Farmers who have been cultivating and irrigating that land can't buy it. The investors bought the Maxwell grant to re-sell at a profit, and they'll sell land almost anywhere else, but not in that part of the country. Have you ever wondered why?"

"Sure," Sheriff Willard answered. "Mr. Springs is gonna bring up more cattle from Texas and he wants to graze them over there."

"Huh-uh." Lawton shook his head. "That's what they've been saying, but it doesn't hold water. Take a look at the deeds and records of land transactions in the county clerk's office. They did sell some of that country. But only as a reward for a favor."

No one spoke for a moment. Lawton cleared his throat again. Then the girl asked, "What do you think, Lawton?"

"That territory is worth more than they figured at first. It's worth a lot of money. It's too valuable to plow up or graze cattle on. One of these days, in the next few years, some men are going to get lousy rich off that land.

"That is," he added, "if they can kick the nesters off."

Another pause, another swallow.

"How, Lawton?" Annie's brown eyes were wide. Her father was listening without blinking. The sheriff was staring at him with a puzzled look on his face.

"How?" Lawton said. "Coal."

He looked at their faces to see if they understood.

It was James C. Gordon who spoke next. "Coal? We've known there was some fossil fuel there. The sawmill has been firing the steam engine with it and some of the settlers have even burned it in their stoves. So . . . I don't understand."

Lawton shifted his weight from one foot to the other before explaining. "You've heard about the railroads coming to Trinidad? Everyone is talking about it. I heard just yesterday that the railroad has got to Cheyenne and is heading south to Denver. Everybody is talking about how it will come to Trinidad. In fact, there's talk that two railroads will come to Trinidad. If that's so—and it must be—what do railroad steam engines use a lot of?"

Annie gasped, "Coal."

Her father said it too, "Coal. They'll buy it by the hundreds of tons. Thousands of tons. It's better fuel than wood and . . ." He paused, thinking, then, "What makes you think there is a huge supply of coal there?"

"They've been drilling holes in the ground, checking. There's coal under the land Baylor bought and there's coal where the Watkins family has been farming. I'm betting there's coal all over that territory."

He looked at their faces again. They were thinking about what he'd just said. Letting it soak in.

"Gosh," said Annie.

Her father turned pensive, frowning at the floor, rubbing his chin. When he spoke, he spoke carefully, thoughtfully. "You're right, Mr. Coop. There will be a railroad in Trinidad within a few years. That's inevitable. This town is on a trade route that has been used for a hundred years or more. There definitely will be a railroad through here, and probably soon. And, yes, I too have heard rumors that two railroads will converge here. But even if only one comes, the demand for coal will be terrific. Coal will be a very valuable commodity. If what you say is true, that there is a large deposit of fossil fuels near Trinidad, this city is going to grow and prosper. It's going to be one of the major cities of the west."

Lawton kept quiet.

Annie added: "Coal. Black gold. It really could be as valuable as gold. Well," she added quickly, "not as valuable as refined gold, but I'll bet a ton of coal will be worth as much as a ton of high-grade gold ore."

Everyone was looking at her now. She continued, "Gold ore has to be milled, refined, run through an extensive and expensive process to separate the gold from the worthless minerals. But coal . . . why coal can be dug up, loaded in wagons and hauled right to the railroads. Every ounce of it."

"And they won't have to haul it very far," her father added.

Everyone was quiet again, trying to comprehend all the possibilities. The potential was so great that it was hard to comprehend.

"It must be true," James C. Gordon said, speaking low, as if to himself. "A lot of people know there is fossil fuel out there, but how many realize the value of it? And what it will mean for this town? Mr. Coop," he looked up at Lawton, "you just realized something that we all should have realized. Somehow it didn't enter my mind. It should have. I . . ."

"It's because I've been doing a lot of thinking about what's going on over there," Lawton said. "I've seen the test holes they drilled. I had a reason for thinking about it and asking a lot of questions."

"Yes." Annie Gordon's brown eyes were wide. "If Baylor had held on to his six hundred acres, he'd soon be rich."

"Yeah," Lawton agreed, "but he'd have been just plain lucky. He didn't know anything about any coal. He was planning to run some cattle over there."

Sheriff Horace Willard had been quiet for the past few minutes, but now he fixed his pale blue eyes on Lawton, a frown on his face. "That," he said, "brings us back to Baylor Coop and the fact of murder and robbery, both committed by said Baylor Coop."

"No," Lawton said. "You're wrong. First, there were two murders, not one. And Baylor didn't do either one of them."

Chapter Twenty-Five

"What?" Annie Gordon gasped. "Did you say Baylor idn't do it?" She was excited. "Tell us, Lawton."

Lawton tried to talk on, but his voice was about to give ut. He had to clear his throat again, and he swallowed hard.

"I'll get you some more water," Annie said, speaking apidly. "I'll get you anything. Whiskey, if you want it."

"Just water," he said.

She ran to the back of the room, pumped furiously, half-an back, carrying a cup of water, spilling some of it. She atched impatiently as he drank and cleared his throat gain. "Go on, Lawton. Please."

"All right," he said. "I'm not used to talking so much, ut . . . well, let me back up a step."

They were listening. Watching his face and listening.

"Uh, let's see, uh, when they realized they'd made a istake selling six hundred acres to Baylor they decided to et it back. He wouldn't sell it back. So they decided to get it ack anyway. Sheriff Spates was allowed in on it. They let im buy a hundred acres of coal land and he agreed to help em get everybody off that territory. What he did was, he ent to the county clerk's office, on a day that Orville ackson was at home sick, and took the records of the land ansaction, the recorded deed to Baylor's land. He could do that, being sheriff. He could go anywhere in the courthouse in the county clerk's office or anywhere else.

"Then he went to Baylor's place and told him he'd have to go, that the land didn't belong to him. Baylor knew better. That was probably late in the day, after the courthouse was closed. Baylor waited until next day and went to the clerk's office. When he saw the clerk wasn't there, he went to the clerk's house. Mrs. Willis asked Mr. Jackson if he would talk to Baylor and Mr. Jackson said he would."

Lawton straightened up, wanted to massage his hips, the part of his anatomy that had been pressed against the desk, couldn't in the presence of the girl, shifted his weight from one foot to the other.

"Orville Jackson assured Baylor that his deed was recorded and he had nothing to worry about, so Baylor went on back to his cabin. Well, that afternoon, Sheriff Spate went out to Baylor's place again and talked to him like a father to a son. He promised that if he'd come to town with him they'd go to the courthouse and get everything settled. It was probably just a misunderstanding. Baylor believed him. Probably because he wanted to believe him. He didn't want any trouble. He, uh, had got acquainted with Annie here and he might have been thinking about settling down."

Glancing at Annie, he saw that her face had turned red. "Well," he added quickly, "Maybe I shouldn't say that. I don't know if that's so. Uh, anyway, Baylor went with him peacefully. They no more than got to town, when Baylor found himself looking up the barrels of a half-dozen guns. They were waiting for him. If they'd tried to get tough out there on Baylor's place, he'd have made a fight of it and some of them would have got hurt or killed. So they laid a trap for him at the courthouse. He didn't have a chance. They locked him up in the town jail.

"But the sheriff had another job to do. He had to make sure Orville Jackson didn't spill the beans. And that's just what he did. He killed Orville Jackson."

Horace Willard exploded, "Now just a minute. Just hold on there, mister. Orville Jackson died of the consumption. Everybody knows that."

"Nope." Lawton was sure of himself. "Everybody knew he was a sick man and didn't have long to live. Orville Jackson himself knew that. But Sheriff Spates and his scheming partners couldn't wait. The county clerk had to be shut up immediately if not sooner. Sheriff Spates killed Orville Jackson."

"How?" Horace Willard barked the word. "You'd better explain yourself, mister."

"How? Well, I'll tell you how. I broke into Bill Spates's house the other night and I found a half-empty bottle of mercury. Do you know what mercury is? It's the same thing as quicksilver. I'll bet every sourdough who has found any gold at all has some quicksilver around. They use it to separate small amounts of gold dust from worthless sand. It's easy to get. And it can kill a man."

Lawton had to shift his weight again. He took another sip from the tin cup. "Bill Spates went to Orville Jackson's house that night, soon after Baylor was locked up, and gave him a drink of water when he started coughing. But first he put a few drops of quicksilver in the water. It didn't kill Mr. Jackson right away. It gave Bill Spates time to leave. He made sure Mrs. Willis saw him leave. Then Orville Jackson went into another coughing fit. Only this time he was choking and gasping as well as coughing. When Mrs. Willis went to check on him next morning she found him dead."

Lawton stopped talking and looked at their faces for a reaction. Their faces were blank. Silence. A heavy freight wagon rattled down Commerce Street. Then Annie said, "It could have happened that way. It really could have."

"Proof," her father said. "You have to have proof. And that would be impossible now."

"Yeah," Horace Willard put in. "You've got no proof of that. You're just running off at the mouth."

Shaking his head sadly, Lawton said, "You're right, I've got no real hard proof. But there is that bottle of mercury in Bill Spates's house, and Mrs. Willis can tell you about Orville Jackson's body when she found him dead, and Doctor Bromley can tell you about the symptoms of mercury poisoning. It all fits together.

"Anyway," Lawton went on, "it doesn't make much difference. Bill Spates is dead. You can't hang a dead man."

"Yeah," the sheriff said, "and that leaves Baylor Coop guilty of bank robbery and the murder of Bill Spates."

"Nope. He didn't kill Bill Spates."

Annie asked, breathlessly, "Who did, Lawton?"

Another sip of water. "What happened is Baylor broke out of jail that night. It was easy. Maybe too easy. Maybe they wanted him to bust out. That made him a man on the dodge, and that put him out of everybody's way. Baylor headed for the hills and hid out. But he couldn't forget it. He knew he'd been cheated. It gnawed on his insides. He couldn't let them get away with it. If he couldn't get his land back, he could at least get back the money he paid for it. That's when he decided to rob the bank."

"Whoa, wait a minute, mister. What did the bank have to do with it?"

"Benjamin Mock is president of the bank. He is a stockholder in the land company. He manages the sale of the land. He was the man who schemed with Bill Spates to get Baylor and the other settlers off the valuable part of the Maxwell grant. Baylor knew that. He knew he'd been cheated, and he knew it had to be Benjamin Mock who was responsible. After all, it was Benjamin Mock who sold him the land, and then Benjamin Mock lied and denied selling it to him. Benjamin Mock had to be the big gun in the whole scheme. Sheriff Spates was just carrying out orders."

Now he had to stop talking for a moment. That last speech took it all out of him.

"You're making some serious accusations there, mister.

192

You'd better know what you're talking about."

Lawton gasped, cleared his throat, took a drink of water, went to the pump and pumped more water, drank it, came back. When he tried to talk again a strangling noise came out. He cleared his throat and tried again.

"Baylor knew. And he wasn't about to let the scheming sonofabuck get by with it. That's why he robbed the bank. Not to clean out the safe, but to get back his nine hundred dollars or whatever amount it was. He did exactly what Mrs. Willis and Benjamin Mock said he did, he put a gun to Mock's nose and marched him to the bank. There, he made him open the safe. He took his nine hundred and left. But . . ."

They were silent again. Even Sheriff Willard was quiet, waiting for him to go on.

"Benjamin Mock saw a chance to fill his pockets with other folks' money. As soon as Baylor made his getaway, he started stuffing a sack with everything in the safe. While all this was going on, Mrs. Willis was hurrying as fast as her feet could carry her to the sheriff. Sheriff Bill Spates came running up at the wrong time. He didn't see Baylor and Baylor didn't see him. Baylor was gone. What he saw was Benjamin Mock robbing the safe. Mr. Mock had a gun somewhere in the bank. He grabbed it and shot the sheriff through the heart." Lawton paused. He suddenly felt very tired. Talking was hard work. He leaned back against the desk and put his hands on the desk behind him. He said:

"It was easy to put the blame on my brother."

There. It was out. He'd told it all. He wanted to sit down but there was no place to sit. If he'd been outside he'd have sat on the ground, anywhere just to get off his feet. But it was a relief to get it all said.

Only it wasn't all said. James C. Gordon had a question. A very important question. He asked quietly, "Mr. Coop, how did you come to that conclusion?"

With a weary sigh, Lawton answered, "According to what

193

I was told, some nineteen thousand dollars was taken from the safe of the Merchants Bank of Las Animas County. Two days later Benjamin Mock deposited eighteen thousand dollars in his personal account in the First National Bank of Pueblo."

Annie finished it for him, her voice tinged with sarcasm, "And where do you think he got the money? One guess."

No one took a guess. But James C. Gordon nodded his head and said simply, "Uh-huh."

Lawton had to get some air. Walking stiffly, he went out the door and stood on the boardwalk, inhaled deeply. Again he thought of Mary and the baby and wished he could saddle up and head south immediately. Sleep somewhere in the Raton Mountains and be on his way again before sunup. He'd push the horses hard, but they'd survive and get a long rest at home. But he couldn't leave yet. He hadn't really accomplished much.

Yeah, he'd figured out what had happened to Baylor and why, but he hadn't proved it. In a court of law, with the lawmen doing a good job of investigating, it could be proven that everything he said was true. Most of it, anyway. The important parts. But he couldn't wait around for that. Maybe he could leave and come back later. If there was a trial, he could come back.

No, there wouldn't be a trial without Baylor and Baylor was . . . no telling where. Somehow he had to let Baylor know.

He was joined by Annie, who put her hand on his arm and looked into his face. "You've uncovered the truth, Lawton. I know it. I've always known Baylor didn't do everything he was accused of."

Without looking at her, he said, "Yeah."

"Will you come back inside, Lawton? Please. We have to talk."

Talk. That's what he was tired of. But she was right. It wasn't over. There was more to do. Reluctantly, he went back inside. Sheriff Willard was still sitting in the chair, fingering his moustache. James C. Gordon was still standing. Annie spoke:

"We can't let it end here. First of all, I want it known that I am very happy to learn that Baylor Coop is not guilty of murder. In my mind, he is not guilty of anything. Second, we've got a—excuse my language—but we've got a hell of a story here."

"Well now . . ." Her father was frowning at the floor, rubbing his chin. "We can't just run off at the press. We've got a strong case, but until it has been proven in a court of law, we can't, uh . . ."

Annie interrupted, "Yes, we can." She turned to Sheriff Willard. "What you have to do is go to Pueblo and see that bank account for yourself, as a public official. That is very important evidence. Then you have to talk to Mrs. Willis and Doctor Bromley and find out whether it is possible that Orville Jackson was poisoned, and then . . ."

Now she was interrupted. "Are you telling me how to do my job, young lady?"

"Suggesting," she said quickly. "Only suggesting. But . . . we are going to print a story about all this, and I would hate to have to report that the sheriff, uh . . ."

Horace Willard got the message. To Lawton he asked, "Are you sure about that bank account? He could have deposited some of the land company's money, you know."

"Huh-uh," Lawton said. "First, if it was company money he would have deposited it in the local bank. Second, it was deposited to Benjamin Mock's personal account. Why would the president of one bank put his personal money in another?"

"How did you know about his personal account?" It was James C. Gordon asking.

"I got a peek, just a peek, at one of his personal papers and

195

I saw the account number. That's why I went to Pueblo, to find out more about it. And I also got a peek at one of Sheriff Spates's papers and he was doing business at the same Pueblo bank."

"All right." Sheriff Horace Willard stood. "But while you were talking I saw the northbound stage go by. I'll have to wait until tomorrow. And, yeah, I'll go see Mrs. Willis and the doctor."

"Good," Annie said. "In the meantime, we have got news."

"Well now." James C. Gordon was still frowning at the floor. "We can't just, uh . . ."

"Why not? Sheriff Spates is dead and we can't libel the dead. As for Benjamin Mock, we'll have to give him a chance to rebut. I'll go see him."

"He's not here," Lawton said. "I saw him on the northbound stage yesterday. He's no doubt found out by now that I was asking questions about his bank account, and there's no telling what he'll do."

"Bully." Annie was excited again. "If he skips the country, that will make it an even better story. But . . ." Her enthusiasm was suddenly dampened. "We won't know for several days." She turned to her father. "What can we do, Dad? We have to do something."

"Well now, we can't print news that we can't substantiate." He continued frowning at the floor and rubbing his chin. "But you're right. We can't sit on this. We've got to print something."

"How about a story on the coal deposits?" Annie said. "We can't say just how much coal is there, but others know there is coal. And we can point out what it will mean to this town when the railroads get here. As for the bank robbery, we can point out the fact that Mr. Mock deposited a large amount of money in his personal account in Pueblo two days after the robbery. Lawton wasn't mistaken about that, and it can be proven. The bank records won't be destroyed."

"That," her father argued, "is directing suspicion at a very

196

nportant man."

"So be it. If he has a logical explanation, we can print that a the next edition. But meanwhile, I think the people of Las Animas County have a right to know everything that has appened and is happening. And that is our job."

James C. Gordon considered that quietly. He walked, ead down, to the opposite end of the room, seemed to study ae cases of type and the flatbed press, walked back, frowned t the floor.

It was his decision, and everyone waited for it. Watched is face and waited.

He stood before them, untied the cravat at his throat and arted rolling up his shirtsleeves. "Well, what are you anding there for? We've got a paper to get out."

"Whooee," Annie yelled. "Boy, are we gonna set this town n its ear."

Chapter Twenty-Six

Lawton was caught up in the excitement. "Can I help? What can I do?"

"Can you set type?" Gordon asked.

"I never saw the stuff before, but I can read."

"Can you read backwards?" Annie asked.

"Sure. Not as fast as you two, but I can do it."

"All right," Gordon said. "We can use all the help we can get. It will take all night to get the story set and to roll off fifty papers, but by sunup tomorrow we'll have a special edition that will be the talk of the whole state."

"Where do I start?"

"Annie, go to the house and fix something to eat. Bring some bread and preserves or whatever we've got. We'll eat while we work. Mr. Coop, if you want to help, you can hand me the type as I ask for it. It's arranged alphabetically in the cases. I'm not going to take time to write the story. I'll compose it as I set type."

Sheriff Willard stood. "I'm gonna go see Mrs. Willis and then the doctor, and I'll be back."

He was ignored as Annie left on the run. James C. Gordon went to the cases of type, and Lawton followed him wondering what to do.

"Let's see now." The publisher stood over one of two

198

atbed chases, the one that already contained large type at
e top which said: "Las Animas Gazette." The chase was di-
ded into four columns. "If you will stand right there, Mr.
oop, by that type-case and hand me the, uh, letters as I
k for them, we'll get started. First the date. Make it tomor-
w's date, which will be July 2."

Annie was right. He not only had to read upside down, he
d to read backwards. He found a capital J and a lower case
 then an l and finally a y. "Put them right there under the
me plate," Gordon said. It took a while, but Lawton got
e letters in the right place. Lordy, he thought, if it takes this
ng, I'll be standing here a week. But the publisher was
ready setting his story in type, working with quick fingers.
 Reading upside down, Lawton made out the words
rinidad is d-e-s-t destined . . ." Then he remembered he as
pposed to be setting type, not reading, and he asked,
Vhat's next?"

"Start with the end of the sentence, Mr. Coop. Give me the
rds "of the west."

"Sure. But call me Lawton. My dad was Mr. Coop."

"Lawton it is."

He found the type faces to form the words and set them in
e right-hand column of the chase. Gordon had to move
em over and rearrange one word, but he thanked Lawton.
 Annie came back, half-running, carrying a loaf of bread
d a jar of plum preserves. "Dinner is served," she said.
nly you have to serve yourself." She sliced the bread,
eared preserves on a slice and handed it to her father. He
 with one hand and worked with the other. Lawton took a
ce and tried to eat and work. He was ashamed of his
wness when he saw Annie grabbing type from the cases
d placing it in another column.

Without looking up, Gordon said, "I'll compose the lead
ry, Annie, and you write a sidebar about the bank
bbery. But be careful how you word it. We don't want to
ke a public apology."

"I don't think we have to worry about that," she said. "And now is my chance to try writing skinny. I mean, use no more words than is absolutely necessary."

"Yeah," her father agreed, "this is not the time to be wordy."

They worked on, Lawton managing to set the last two or three words of each sentence for Gordon. He discovered that one case of type contained lead slugs with complete words but only the most common words, such as "and" and "the." Annie was busy setting her own story. While they worked Sheriff Horace Willard came in.

"It was like you said, Coop. Mrs. Willis told me how she found Orville Jackson's body, and Doc Bromley said he could have been poisoned with quicksilver. We'll never be able to prove it, but we can prove something with a copy of that bank statement from Pueblo. I've got a deputy on his way."

"I didn't know you had a deputy," Annie said.

"I've got a volunteer. I gave him a deputy's badge, the one Sheriff Spates's deputy wore, and a note with my signature. He can change horses at the stage stops, and he'll get there tonight."

"That's good," James C. Gordon murmured without looking up.

The sheriff was ignored for a moment, and he sat at the desk and watched them work. Soon he stood, looked out the door and said, "Stage just pulled in. Benjamin Mock was the first one to light."

"Oh-oh," said Annie, her head coming up. "I'll have to go and see him and let him tell his side of the story. We have to be fair." She wiped her hands on a towel hanging from the side of the flatbed chase, ran her hands over her hair.

"I'll go with you," Lawton said. "He's not the gentleman he seems to be."

"No. Best I go by myself. He'd have nothing to gain by harming me. I'll go right now." She grabbed a sheaf of paper and a lead pencil and hurried out the door.

Lawton watched her go, worried. Her father looked up too, worry wrinkles on his forehead. "She's always been a little too independent. She's at the age where I can't tell her what to do." He shook his head sadly. "Pity the man who marries her. He'll have to be strong."

At that, Lawton had to grin. It brought Baylor to his mind. Baylor was strong enough for her. Then back to work. "What's next?"

Forty-five miutes later, Annie came back. "He denied it, of course. He said the money he deposited in the Pueblo bank is company money. He said he chose the Pueblo bank because he discovered his own bank is too easy to rob."

"Not a very good advertisement for his own bank," her father said, glancing up at her.

"No, and I don't believe him. He suddenly has a kind of sneaky look about him. I agree with Lawton, he's not the gentleman he appears to be. There's something about him, something suspicious. But, well, I'll tell his side of the story and let the public believe him or disbelieve him."

By dark, Lawton's fingers and eyes were tired. Annie and her father lighted a half-dozen lamps and worked on. Lawton kept going too. Sheriff Horace Willard left, was gone an hour and came back. He had a loaf of fresh bread with him and a jar of apple butter.

"I'd help too, but I'm no good at printing a newspaper," he said. "Howsomever, I did fetch some chuck."

Again, they ate while they worked. Gordon's story was nearing completion, and Annie was setting type as fast as her fingers would go, barely pausing to think between sentences. Lawton tried to read the top of her story, and was surprised and a little shocked to recognize his name. He made out a few more words:

"Lawton Coop, brother of accused murderer and bank robber Baylor Coop, believes his brother is innocent of any wrongdoing."

"Well," he said, "that's the first time I ever saw my name in a newspaper, but it's the truth."

Annie suddenly stopped working long enough to go to the door, look out at the black night, then close and bolt the door. "I'm probably imagining things," she said, "but Benjamin Mock gave me the creeps. I have a feeling . . ."

That was when the first shot boomed out.

Everyone straightened up suddenly, startled, speechless. The shot shattered glass in the building's high front window and the bullet pinged off the brick wall near the ceiling. Annie spun around facing the window, shocked.

Lawton got a glimpse of a face at the window, a face with a six-gun beside it. He yelled, "Get down," and yanked the Army Colt out of its holster. "Hit the floor."

Annie and her father dropped to the floor just as another bullet screamed off the edge of a type-case and thudded into the far wall.

"God damn," Sheriff Willard yelled. "Some damn body is shooting."

A volley of shots came through the window then, scattering bullets over the room. Sounding like angry hornets, they ricocheted off the printing equipment and dug furrows in the walls.

Annie's face was white. Gordon was flat on the floor, his arm over his head. The sheriff was on one knee, aiming his six-gun at the window.

Lawton snapped three shots at the face in the window, but the face had disappeared. The sheriff's gun bellowed too.

The shooting stopped.

"Get the lights," Lawton said. He stood and started to blow out the nearest lamp.

"No." James C. Gordon was getting to his feet. "That's what they want. We've got to keep working."

"You can't keep working," the sheriff yelled, looking back at them.

202

"What do you think, Annie?" the publisher asked his daughter.

"Yes." She stood. "They're trying to stop us. We can't let them do it."

"You'll get killed," Horace Willard argued.

"We can't let them stop us."

"All right." Lawton stood too. "Sheriff, keep an eye on that window. Don't let anybody take a look through. I'll watch the back window."

Gordon said quietly, "Do you really want to keep working, Annie?"

"I'm working." And she was, standing over the chase, fingers flying.

A bullet came through the back window then, scattering glass and whining dangerously across the room. Lawton took a quick look through the broken glass, saw only darkness. He fired a shot anyway just to let everyone out there know the people inside were capable of fighting back.

It was quiet again. Both Lawton and the sheriff took cartridges from their gunbelts and reloaded their six-guns. Lawton wished for the Spencer he'd left in his cabin at the wagon camp, and he wished for more .44 ammunition for his Colt. From here on he'd have to make every shot count. No more shooting into the dark.

The Gordons continued working, and finally James C. Gordon said, "Done. Annie, how about you?"

"Almost."

"I'll ink the press."

The shooting started again. Lead slugs ricocheted and sang their deadly song around the room. But the windows were high enough that the shooters would have to get close, get their faces up to them, to see inside. Their faces, when they did look in, made good targets. So they stayed back and scattered bullets in hopes someone would be hit by a ricochet. The Gordons bent as low as they could and kept on working.

Muttering under his breath, Lawton said, "Come on, you yellow-livered sonsofbitches. Show yourselves. Just once."

James C. Gordon raised the huge drum that was suspended over one end of the chase and poured ink into a series of inking rollers. "How're you doing, Annie?"

"Almost done." She didn't look up.

A face appeared at the window near Lawton, but only for a half-second. It disappeared before he could aim at it. A shotgun blast tore through the window and lead pellets knocked out one of the lights and pinged off the type-cases. Three seconds later, four shots were fired through the front window, driving Sheriff Willard back behind the desk. He returned the fire, but he had no target to shoot at.

Lawton muttered, "This just won't do. They can stand out there in the dark and shoot at us all night. Sooner or later they're gonna hit somebody." He yelled at the sheriff, "What do you think we ought to do?"

"I think we ought to blow out the lamps and take cover."

"Keep your eyes on that window."

"Done," Annie said. "Let's roll the press."

"It's ready," her father said.

Sheriff Willard spoke from behind the desk, "You folks got more guts than I have. In fact, you're crazy."

Lawton said, "Somebody's gonna get killed unless we do something."

Annie stretched a sheet of blank paper onto the chase from a large roll of paper. Her father lowered the drum. "Are we ready to roll?" he asked.

"Roll it."

The publisher pulled a long lever and the drum rolled the length of the chase, pressing the paper down onto inked type faces. When he rolled it back, Annie picked up the paper and turned it over. "That's page one."

"That'll be our only page for this edition."

"Yes," Annie said with a half-smile, "but isn't it a booger." She stretched more paper onto the chase. Her father pulled

204

he handle.

With an explosion that shook the building, a shotgun blast tore a hole in the wall just two feet over Gordon's head.

"Lordy," Lawton muttered, "I've got to do something. I an't just stand here by the window and let them kill omebody." He yelled at the sheriff, "Can you see anything ut there?"

"Darker'n a stack of black cats."

"Trade places with me, will you, and watch this window."

"What're you gonna do?"

"I'm going out there."

Chapter Twenty-Seven

They tried to talk him out of it.

"You won't get two steps out the door," Sheriff Horace Willard said.

"Don't get killed for our benefit, Lawton," said Annie Gordon.

"We'll get the paper out in spite of them," said her father.

"Listen," Lawton argued, "that newspaper is for my benefit and Baylor's as much as for anybody else."

Annie said, "Sure, I thought of that too, but . . ."

Another shotgun blast came through the back window and knocked another hole in the wall near where James C. Gordon was working. Two rifle shots came through the front window.

"That does it," Lawton muttered.

"You'll be a perfect target the second you open that door," the sheriff argued.

"No. Here's what to do. Put out the lamps and wait till I get outside before you light them again. In the dark I can slip out."

"Lawton . . ." Before she could finish what she started to say, he blew out two of the lamps. The sheriff blew out another and her father blew out the last one. It was dark. So dark he had to grope his way to the door.

Sliding the latch back, he whispered, "Give me twenty seconds, then light the lamps again." He pulled the door open, bent low and ran out.

The moon still had its dark side to the earth, and the night was pitch black. But they heard him. He no more than yanked the door closed behind him when a shotgun blast ripped into the door. Had he been standing upright, it would have taken his head off. He didn't wait to see where the blast came from, but ran, bent low, for the corner of the building.

A rifle and a pistol opened up on him. A bullet thunked into the brick side of the building, and another whirred over his head. Once he was around the corner he hit the ground face-down in the weeds of a vacant lot. He heard a man yell:

"He's in the weeds. Shoot in the weeds."

Lawton crawled, first on his stomach, then on his hands and knees. Gunfire boomed, crashed and popped, and bullets hit the ground dangerously close. He crawled until he was on the opposite side of the lot and at the bottom edge of the next-door building. There, he stopped, turned and looked behind him. The dark shadow of a man was coming toward him, barely visible. More gunfire. The man stopped, yelled:

"Wait a minute, God damn it. I'm over here. Hold your God damned fire a minute. I think I know where he is." He continued on toward Lawton.

Lawton had the Army Colt ready, the hammer back. He knew that if he fired the muzzle flash would give away his position, and the guns would open up on him again. He hoped he wouldn't have to shoot. Not yet.

"Hey, they're lightin' the lamps in there."

"God damn. Pour it to 'em."

A dim light illuminated the front window. A man appeared in front of the window. Only his hat and shoulders were visible in the dark. He raised a pistol. Lawton fired two shots, fanning the hammer back on his Colt. The first shot knocked down the man at the window, and the second hit the man who was approaching him.

"Jesus Christ, they got Matson. Pour it to 'em, God damn 'em."

"That feller's over there by the laundry somewhere. Shoot the sonofabitch."

More bullets came Lawton's way. He crawled again. This time toward the street. Glancing up at the newspaper building, he saw that it was well lighted, and he knew the Gordons were rolling the press. While he was watching the front window, he hoped Sheriff Willard was guarding the back one.

On the plank walk now, hugging the front of the laundry, he watched. The window in the newspaper building put out enough light that he could see anything directly in front of it. Two men were pulling another man away, a dead man. Dead or hurt so bad he couldn't stand. They dragged him into the dark. Then one of them knelt under the window, a rifle in his hands. Lawton could see him, knew he was trying to get up enough nerve to stand up straight, aim his rifle at somebody inside and shoot. Couldn't let him do it.

The Army Colt barked again. The rifleman dropped, screaming, "I'm hit. I'm shot. Help me."

Now Lawton stood up and ran. Two shots followed him. Pistol shots. He'd gunned down three men. How many damned more were there in front of the building? Couldn't be many more. One thing was certain, they wouldn't dare show themselves in the light from the window again. Not as long as he was out there. But somebody with a shotgun was blasting through the back window. He had to get around back.

He ran, boots pounding the planks. Another pistol shot. Then he was round the corner of the laundry, heading for the alley. He got there in time to see somebody at the back window. Squatting under it. Raising up with a long gun. Putting the gun to his shoulder.

Without taking time to aim, Lawton fired. He knew he'd

missed. But his shot caused the gunman to spin around and drop to the ground without pulling the trigger. Whoever he was, he was no fool. He quickly got out of the light, kept still and looked to see where Lawton's shot had come from.

Now it was two men facing each other in the dark, one armed with a pistol and the other with a shotgun. Each daring the other to move.

At first Lawton cussed the dark. He couldn't see anybody to shoot at. Then he thanked the Lord for it. They couldn't see him. The best part of it was nobody could rise up to shoot through the window without being seen. Lawton kept his eyes on the window.

Waited. On his belly in the dirt of the alley. Listened and waited. The Colt ready.

Show yourself, you sonofabitch, he muttered under his breath.

And then it occurred to him that he could guard only one end of the building at a time. And he'd asked the sheriff to guard the back window. If he was, then the front window was unguarded. Damn. He'd done something estupido by running back to the alley.

No. That sonofabitch with the shotgun was going to get lucky sooner or later. He had to be stopped, and he could only be stopped from the outside.

No one was shooting now. The town was quiet. Except for the barking dogs. Quiet and dark. What were the townsmen doing? They couldn't help hearing all the gunfire. What could they do? They knew something was happening, somebody was trying to kill somebody, but it was so dark outside they couldn't do a damned thing about it. Just wait for daylight and pick up the bodies.

A pistol shot sounded in front of the building. Another.

Lawton swore under his breath. One of the two windows was unguarded. Which one? He had to do something. He couldn't just wait here. He had to make something happen.

Groping the ground, he found a rock and threw it into the

weeds between the laundry and the newspaper building, hoping it would draw fire. It was an old Indian trick, so old and talked about so much it wouldn't fool anybody. It didn't. Groping again, he found a stick and threw it into the weeds. Heard it hit the ground. Still, it didn't work.

Quiet.

Uh-oh. Something moved. Barely. Over there by the corner of the newspaper building. Something was moving over there.

Watch. Wait.

He couldn't see it. It wasn't moving now. What was it? Had to be a man.

Breathing with shallow breaths, Lawton watched, eyes straining, his finger on the trigger of the Colt.

There. It moved again.

Lawton had the Colt aimed at the spot. Come on, you sonofabitch. He groped for something else to throw. His fingers moved a rock, or something. It was a mistake.

A charge of buckshot hit the ground two feet from his right shoulder. The explosion shattered the quiet.

Lawton fired at the muzzle blast. Cocked the hammer back and fired again. Got up and ran, hit the back of the laundry, bounced off it and ran across the alley.

A second blast. Something pulled at the left side of his shirt. Leveling the Colt, he squeezed the trigger. Nothing. A click on an empty shell casing.

His mind told him two blasts had been fired from the shotgun. It was a double-barreled gun. It was now empty. So was his Colt. Who could reload the fastest?

He could see the man now. He could see a dark spot in the shape of a man. It was moving. Had to get him. Lawton ran. Ran right at him.

Chapter Twenty-Eight

While he ran Lawton expected to be hit with a pistol shot. Surely the man had a pistol. Surely he wouldn't be fool enough to try to reload that shotgun in time to stop him. Would Lawton feel the blast? Would he hear the shot? Or would it kill him instantly? He knew he was doing something dumb, but he ran.

Then he collided with something, something soft. It went down with Lawton on top of it. It cursed and twisted and bucked. Its breath stank. Lawton still had the Colt in his hand. He swung it, hit the ground. Swung it again.

The man was big. Big and strong. He twisted and bucked, and got out from under Lawton. Lawton reached up with his left hand and got hold of cloth. The bib of some overalls. He jumped to his feet and hung onto it. The man cursed, grunted, wheezed. Lawton swung the Colt again. Again and again. It hit something. Another curse. Again.

Then he was swinging the gun at the empty air. The man was down. Lawton dropped to his knees on top of him. Pounded with the gun. Knew he was hitting something. Kept pounding. The man was still.

Now Lawton was cursing. "You sonofabitch, you low-life sonofabitch, you God damned sonofabitch." Cursing and pounding a form in the dark.

Realizing finally that his enemy wasn't moving, Lawton stopped pounding and stopped cursing. Breathing heavily from the exertion, he holstered the Colt, and felt for a face. He found a face, a bearded face, found a gunbelt, a six-gun. Groping the ground around him, he found the shotgun. The shotgun was broken open. He'd caught the gunner in the act of reloading. He threw the gun away.

It was quiet again. Lawton sat on his heels beside the downed man and wondered if he was dead or just knocked out. He wondered if anybody else was in the alley. Then he remembered the front window, and wondered if the sheriff was watching it.

He listened. For at least two minutes, he listened and believed there was no one else at the rear of the building. That left only the front to worry about. Carrying the downed man's six-gun, he walked through the weeds toward the street. At the corner of the building he stopped. The front window was still putting out light. He wanted to look inside, but he didn't dare. If the sheriff was on guard, he'd catch a .44 slug in the face. He wanted to yell and ask if anybody was hurt inside. He didn't dare make a sound and give away his position. All he could do was stay here and wait. Then someone else made a sound.

"Is that you, Bob?"

"Yeah," Lawton whispered.

"I heard old Ansil's scattergun. He must have got 'im."

"Yeah."

"I'm gonna take a look."

"Go ahead."

"Hey, Bob."

"What?"

"What's my name?"

"Shitface."

A pistol popped and a slug whistled over Lawton's head. He used the downed man's six-gun to fire at the flash. He heard footsteps running away. Running down the street.

Then quiet.

Crouching in the weeds beside the newspaper building, Lawton wondered how many more men were over there in the dark. One had just run away. Was he the last of them? How many had he shot? Let's see. Two at the front window and one that was coming toward him in the dark. That's three. Then the one in the alley. He probably wasn't dead, but he had no fight left in him. Four. Plus the one who ran away. Five. Any more?

No way of knowing.

Wait and see. Was anybody hurt inside? He had to find out. Moving as quietly as he could, he worked his way to the door, stood beside it. "Hey, Sheriff. Sheriff Willard. It's Lawton Coop. Anybody hurt in there?"

The voice came through the door. "No. Not bad. They're still working. How many out there?"

"I don't know. Watch the back window, will you? I'll watch the front. I'll have to stay here till daylight."

"I'm watching."

Now he had to move. If there was anybody around, Lawton's position was known. He moved, keeping low, back the way he'd come. Moved just in time. A bullet thunked into the door at the same time a rifle cracked somewhere across the street. There was at least one more man over there. Lawton crawled on his hands and knees across the vacant lot. When he found the laundry building, he crawled to a spot near the corner where he could see the lighted window. There, he sat on the ground with the six-gun on his knees and waited for something to happen.

Waited for daylight.

It was a long time coming. Once, he heard movement across the street and saw a vague shape move. He didn't fire at it. Eyes straining, he tried to watch the alley, but an army could have been standing there without being seen. What was going on inside? The sheriff said nobody was hurt bad. Did that mean somebody was hurt a little? Who? He said they were still working. How many papers had they printed by now? Wait.

Come on, daylight.

At first he wasn't aware of it. Vague shapes began to appear. His butt ached from sitting in one position. He was facing east, straining his eyes. It was a corner of the newspaper building that showed first. A square corner. The alley was still dark. The street was still dark. Then he could see the side of the building. A faint glow was moving up behind the eastern horizon. It outlined the street with dark buildings on each side. A dog barked. Another dog answered. Someone was coming down the street with a lantern. Right down the middle of the street.

Now he could see the hitchracks across the street and the windows of the building, a hardware store. The man with the lantern came on, walking slowly. Nothing else moved. Another lantern appeared away down on the west end of the street, coming this way, bobbing as it was carried. The eastern horizon glowed brighter. He could see the street and the alley. A lump lay in the weeds near the alley. A man. The shotgun shooter. Either dead or near death.

The first man with a lantern was in front of the newspaper building. He stopped, then went to the window and started to look in.

"Hey," Lawton yelled, standing, "don't do that. You might get shot."

The man saw Lawton then, and jumped back. "What . . . what's goin' on here?"

"It's all right," Lawton said. "But stay away from that window." He walked stiffly toward the man.

"I heard shootin'. What the bully hell's goin' on?"

"There was some shooting, all right. But I think it's over

214

ow." He got close to the door and yelled, "Hey, Sheriff, I ⊥ink they're gone."

"Sheriff? Is the sheriff in there?"

"Yeah."

The door opened and Sheriff Horace Willard looked out. You still alive, Coop?"

"Yeah. Are the Gordons all right?"

The sheriff stepped outside. "Mr. Gordon took a piece of ⊥uckshot in the cheek, but he's still going."

"How about Annie?"

"She never even slowed down."

Lawton shook his head in admiration.

"Any dead men out here?"

"I think they carried away their dead. I know I shot at least ⊥ree. There's one in the alley. I don't know if he's dead."

"Sheriff Willard?" The lantern was held up higher. "What ⊥appened? I heard a lot of shootin'." The second citizen ⊥arrying a lantern came up. "What's goin' on? Who done all ⊥e shootin'? Is that you, Sheriff?"

More men appeared on the street, all coming toward the ⊥ewspaper building. "What's goin' on? What was all the ⊥ootin' about?"

"Sounded like Cox's army out here. I couldn't see a ⊥amned thing."

"How many men killed?"

Horace Willard tried to explain, "Just some gunslammers ⊥ying to keep the folks in there from printing their ⊥ewspaper. They're gone now. It's all over, folks."

"The newspaper?"

"Yeah." To Lawton he said, "Let's go have a look at that ⊥nt in the alley."

"Did somebody say Coop? Is that that Coop feller?"

Sheriff Willard answered, "Yeah. He's all right." They ⊥und the man trying to sit up, holding his head in both ⊥ands. The shotgun was in the weeds twenty feet away. ⊥heriff Willard squatted in front of him. "Hurts, huh?"

215

No answer.

Standing, the sheriff said, "We'll get the doc to keep him alive. I want to talk to this jasper."

"I'll get the doctor," someone said, and left.

Lawton said, "I think you know who's behind all this."

"Yup. I'm gonna have to arrest him. I'll do that right now."

"Want some help?"

"Nope. I'll arrest that gentleman myself."

"He's desperate, Sheriff. I'll go with you if you want me to."

Horace Willard was already walking away. "Nope. I'll get him."

The Gordons, Lawton had to see them. He nodded at the man on the ground and said to the townsmen gathered around, "Don't let him get away." At the front door, he pushed it open gently, half-afraid he'd be greeted with gunfire. But the Gordons were rolling the press. James C. Gordon was inking the rollers and pulling the long handle. His left cheek was bloody, and his left shirtsleeve was bloody. Annie Gordon was laying out paper, cutting it and folding it.

When they saw him, Annie smiled. "Almost fifty copies. Wait till you read it, Lawton."

"We're going to stop in a minute," her father said. "This will be enough for the time being."

Looking around the room, Lawton shook his head. It was a battleground. Broken glass littered the floor in front of the two windows. Holes the size of a man's fist had been blasted in the wall over the press. A lamp globe had shattered. The ceiling was pockmarked with bullet holes. Annie's face was streaked with ink, but she appeared to be unhurt. Gordon's wounds appeared to be superficial. Again, Lawton shook his head.

He said, "In my whole put together, I've never even heard of anything like this."

"We got it done," Gordon said. "It took all of us—you and the sheriff and Annie and me. We'd have been helpless without you two."

"We're ready to hit the street now." Annie picked up an armload of newspapers, handed one to Lawton. "Here, read all about it." Gordon picked up an armload of newspapers. "We'll ask for a nickel a copy, but we'll take what we can get."

Before they could get out the door, before Lawton could start reading, Sheriff Horace Willard came in, half-running, breathless.

"He's gone."

"Who?" Annie asked.

"Ben Mock. Cleaned out the bank and hauled out of here."

Chapter Twenty-Nine

A half-dozen townsmen came into the room, looked around, and exclaimed, "Good gawd a-mighty. What the hound dog hell? Beats anything I ever saw. You got some newspapers there, Miss?"

"Yes," said Annie. "Five cents. Read all about it."

A half-dozen coins were shoved into her hands and newspapers were taken from her arm. Another townsman stepped up.

"Mr. Sheriff, did I heard you say something about Benjamin Mock?"

"Yeah. Have you see him?"

"Seen 'im 'bout an hour ago. When it was first light. Goin' west on a sorrel horse. Foggin' it. Carryin' a gunny sack full of somethin'."

"West, huh? Quitting the country. I'll get my horse and get after him."

Lawton said, "I'll go with you."

"Me too," said a townsman. "I'll go," said another.

"Get your horses and meet me out in the street," the sheriff said. "I've got a hunch that banker gent has all the town's money."

"In that case, we sure got to git that jasper," someone said.

Lawton left on the run, heading for the wagon camp. It was too far to run, and he had to slow to a fast walk and get

218

his breath. His dun horse was munching hay when he slipped a bridle over its head and led it out of the stall. "Sorry, old boy. We've got work to do." He saddled up in a hurry, and was about to put his foot in the stirrup, when he remembered the Spencer.

Running again, he slammed open the door to his rented cabin, grabbed the rifle from under the bed and a handful of cartridges from one of his pack panniers. Outside, he almost ran into the camp owner.

"Hey, what the hell was goin' on over there? You in on that? Sounded like the Alamo all over again."

"There was some shooting," Lawton said, hurrying past him. He ran to the horse, gathered the reins and got mounted.

"Well, who was shootin' at who?"

"Read about it in the newspapers." Lawton rode at a gallop out of the camp yard.

There were eight or ten men on horseback, heavily armed, milling in front of the newspaper building. Townsmen and women were arriving from all directions, and the Gordons were selling newspapers as fast as they could collect the money.

"Where's the sheriff?" someone yelled.

"Yeah, where is he? Sure takin' 'im a long time to git his horse."

"Let's go."

"Better wait for the sheriff. He's the law."

"Hey, is that him?"

All heads swiveled to the west. A lone rider was coming, riding at a slow shuffling trot. Riding a mule.

"That's not Willard."

"Who is it?"

"Why, it's, uh, aw hell, it's that old sourdough."

"It's him, all right."

All eyes watched as Weepy Willows rode toward them. He was carrying a burlap bag on the saddle in front of him, and had a six-gun in a holster hanging from the saddle horn. His

Henry rifle was in a boot under his left leg. When he saw all the people staring at him he pulled up. His mule didn't like the smell of town, and was shuffling its feet and waggling its long ears. The sheriff rode up, stopped and stared.

"Hey, Willows," the sheriff yelled. "Come over here."

The old man with the white beard and wet eyes kicked the mule with spurless boot heels, and the mule moved forward, ears twitching. "Yeah?" he said, cautiously.

"Did you just come in from the west?"

"Yup."

"Did you see anybody?"

"Yup."

"Was it that banker, Benjamin Mock?"

The mule tried to turn around and leave. "Whoa, Jennifer." Willows plow-lined the mule back, facing the crowd. "Yup."

"How far?"

"Six or eight mile, I reckon."

"Straight west?"

"Southwest."

The sheriff spoke to the crowd, "Maybe we can catch him before he gets over the mountains."

"Let's ride."

"No hurry," Willows said. "Whoa, Jennifer."

"What? Why?"

"He ain't goin' far."

The sheriff reined his horse up close to Willows. "Why do you say that, Mr. Willows?"

"He's afoot."

"Afoot?"

"Yup."

"Well, uh . . ."

"Listen." Lawton got into the conversation. "Maybe we'd better have a talk. Somewhere private. What do you say, let's go in the newspaper building. Mr. Willows, you, sheriff, and me. Somebody hold Mr. Willows's mule."

"I'll hold 'er." A pair of hands reached for the bridle reins as Weepy Willows swung down, hanging onto the burlap bag.

"What's in the sack, Weepy?"

He didn't answer, but followed Sheriff Willard and Lawton onto the boardwalk and through the door. Inside, Lawton closed the door. "What happened, Mr. Willows? Sit down in that chair."

Willows sat, wiped a shirtsleeve across his eyes, blinked. "Wa-al, I was headin' for town, plannin' to wet my swaller pipe and buy some grub, and I seen this feller ridin' hell for leather right at me. Wasn't much after first light. He was ridin' like the 'Paches was on his tail. Didn't have no respect for that horse a-tall. Good lookin' horse too. But no horse can keep up that way forever."

He paused, swallowed, wiped his eyes again. Blinked.

Lawton and the sheriff waited for him to go on.

"Wa-al, shore 'nuff, the horse went down. Stumbled and went down. Pitched that feller right over his head. The horse was done for. Never twitched a muscle again. Wa-al, I went over to see if that feller was hurt, although I didn't care a hell of a lot. Feller'd run a horse down like that oughtta get hurt."

Another pause. Lawton could sympathize with him. He'd gone through a long-winded story himself the day before.

"Care for a drink of water, Mr. Willows?"

"Could use a drink of whiskey."

"I'll get you one," the sheriff said, "as soon as you tell us what happened."

"Sombitch throwed a gun on me. He was some skinned up but able to stand up and point that damn pistol at me. Told me to git off my mule or he'd blow my goddamn head off. Wa-al, I got down and done like he tole me to. I didn't wanta git my head blowed off."

Weepy wiped his eyes again, blinked and held up the burlap bag. "He was hangin' onto this sack like he was afraid I'd run off. He tried to git on my mule and hang onto this sack and his pistol at the same time. I was just standin' there watchin'.

"Wa-al, old Jennifer, she don't care much for strangers anyhow, and she snorted like a steam engine and went straight up. That sombitch turned a double fart-knocker and lit flat on his back. He wasn't dead but he had the hound dog shit knocked out of 'im."

"What's in the sack, Mr. Willows?"

"Money. I sneaked a look. Greenbacks. U.S. Gov'ment money. Must be more'n a thousand dollars in here. Here." He handed the bag to the sheriff, and stood. "Now, I ain' done nothin' that's agin the law and I'm gonna git me a drink of whiskey."

Sheriff Willard smiled. Lawton smiled. Sheriff Willard laughed. "No, Mr. Willows, you haven't done anything against the law. In fact, you've been a big help to the law. In fact, I think you just saved this town its money. In fact, I'll bet this sack is holding not only all the money from the bank's safe, but just about all the money that was stolen from the bank last fall. You bet, I'll buy you a drink. Come on. Let's go have a shot of whiskey, then some breakfast, and then I'll go pick that gentleman up. Is that his gun you've got on your saddle?"

"Yup."

"Mr. Willows." Lawton held out his hand to shake. "I might not see you again. Thanks a lot. I owe you. This town owes you."

"Yup." They shook. "Say, have you heard from your brother?"

"No. But wherever he is, he's all right now."

Outside, the sheriff told the townsmen to go home. Benjamin Mock was as good as caught, he told them, and the bank's money was safe. Annie had sold all her papers, all but one. She handed it to Lawton. He read hastily. The story was there. Two stories. One told about the coal deposits on the west of Trinidad and what it meant to the town. The other with Ann Gordon's byline, told about last fall's bank robbery and murder, and who committed it. The story named names.

"We didn't pull any punches," Annie said. "If there ever was any doubt, it was dispelled last night when the shooting started. We knew who was behind it, and we named him."

"Yeah," Lawton said, folding the paper, putting it in a shirt pocket. "But . . ."

She interrupted, "You're wondering whether this will help Baylor. I think it will. I'm going over to the telegraph office and send this story to the Pueblo and Denver papers. From Denver it will be telegraphed to newspapers all over the west. Baylor will see it and he'll come back."

Smiling, Lawton said, "You and your dad are the best friends Baylor ever had. He'd be a fool not to come back."

"How about some breakfast, Lawton?"

"Well." He looked at the rising sun. "If I get started now I can be over the mountains by dark. Or almost."

"Leave? You're leaving?"

"Yeah." That terrible feeling of urgency was back. He'd done all he could here, and it was time to go. He had to go. "Got to get home. I can eat some bread on the way. I'll buy some chuck at the toll gate, at Mr. Wootton's place."

"I'm sorry to see you leave, Lawton, but I understand."

"Goodby, Annie. Thanks. Say goodby to your dad. I hope to see you again."

"I hope to see you again too, Lawton. Good luck." He walked to his horse, got mounted. She yelled, "Give my regards to your wife."

It took four days to get to White Lake, New Mexico Territory. About noon on the fourth day, a southbound stage passed him. The fresh harness horses traveled at a fast trot, even a gallop at times. Lawton wrinkled his nose at the tail of dust left by the stage and kept his tired horses going at a slow steady trot. "Not much farther, fellers," he said. "Then you can put your noses in some good feed and rest for a week. Two weeks."

He didn't plan to stop in White Lake, but when he heard

his name called, he reined up. Mrs. Ables, the postmistress, was behind him on the plank walk, waving at him. "Yoo-hoo, Lawton." She was waving an envelope. He turned his horses around and went back to her.

"It's a letter from Baylor," she said. "It just now came in on the stage. He was in Denver in Colorado, but he posted this in Pueblo in Colorado just four days ago. Isn't that wonderful?"

Without dismounting, Lawton took the letter from her hand. "Thanks, Mrs. Ables." He read it while he rode. "Well, I'll be damned. He was in Denver, then he went to Pueblo. Hell, we were both in Pueblo at the same time and didn't know it. I'll be damned. Not far now, old fellers. We'll soon be home."

Mary saw him coming. She was standing in the yard where she had planted some green bushes and flowers, shading her eyes with her hand, looking up the road. When she recognized him, she let out a yell and hurried to meet him. Hurried as fast as she could, pushing her stomach ahead of her. Lawton grinned. She was still pregnant. He booted the horses into a gallop, and hit the ground running while the horses went on.

Careful not to hurt the baby, he hugged her and looked into her wide gray eyes. Her smiling gray eyes. And now Mrs. Coop was running from the big house, running pretty good for a woman her age. Then he had his arms around both women.

They hugged and kissed and patted each other, and his mother pulled back, a worry frown on her wrinkled face. "Baylor?"

He grinned. "Baylor's fine. Here's a letter from him. He's gonna stop in Trinidad in Colorado for a couple of days to see somebody, somebody very important."

"And then?"

"Baylor's coming home."